BALLET

SCHOOL

Samira's Garden

Written by
Fiona Macdonald

Illustrated by
Annaliese Stoney

SCRIBO
a SALARIYA *imprint*

Introduction

Rosewood Ballet School

BALLET

SCHOOL

Samira's Garden

SCRIBO

Published in Great Britain in MMXVII by
Scribblers, an imprint of
The Salariya Book Company Ltd
25 Marlborough Place,
Brighton BN1 1UB
www.salariya.com

© The Salariya Book Company Ltd
MMXVII

ISBN 978-1-912006-62-5

1 3 5 7 9 8 6 4 2

A CIP catalogue record for this book
is available from the British Library.

Printed and bound in China.

Visit
www.salariya.com
for our online catalogue and
free fun stuff.

Hi! I'm Willow – Willow Emily Maria Johnson, if you really want to know – and I'm nine years old. I live in a small messy house in a big busy city with my mum and my dad and my kid brother Jake. Mum often jokes that Dad's racing bikes live with us too; Dad's crazy about cycling and is always bringing bits of his machines indoors to clean and repair. Mum's always very busy and sometimes rather tired. She's kind and clever and studying to be a nurse. There are heaps of medical books and papers all over the house. Jake's OK really, though he teases me too much and his pet spiders are scary; I hate them! My very best friend in the whole world is Samira. She's the same age as me and she lives next door and we go to school together.

And me? I'm small and mousy-haired and quiet-looking, although Mum says I can make an awful lot of noise for my size. I quite like ordinary school – but I'm passionate about ballet. I dream of being a ballerina, but I don't know if I'll ever be good enough. I practise every day and go to ballet classes twice a week at Rosewood Ballet School. This book is about me and the school and the ballet friends I've made there.

First, let me tell you about the school. 'Rosewood' sounds pretty, doesn't it? Like flowers growing among the trees. Or like the enchanted forest in Sleeping Beauty. I've watched that ballet lots of times on DVD, but I'd love to see it performed live in a theatre. The story's so romantic! There's this magic scene where the Princess falls asleep for 100 years and the roses grow up and hide her ...

Sorry! I should also have said that I'm a terrible daydreamer. Well, actually, it's not terrible, it's lovely! When things get boring I just switch off and think about music and dancing. Did I say that Mum is also helping me to learn to read music and play the recorder? I'm not very good at that, but it's important for ballerinas to know about music, so I keep trying.

Anyway, back to Rosewood Ballet School. I can tell you that it's definitely not pretty to look at. There are no trees or flowers in sight. Instead, it's a big concrete building on the edge of a car park close to the railway station. I think it used to be offices. Downstairs, there are two big ballet studios and some changing rooms; upstairs there are smaller practice rooms, a huge cupboard full of sheet music and DVDs, and several offices. Outside, it's getting very shabby. Once, the concrete was painted white, but the city air has turned that dirty grey and some of the paint is peeling.

Inside? Inside! Ah, well that's another story! To me and my ballet friends, stepping into Rosewood Ballet School is like walking into a dream factory. Once we've changed into dancing clothes and started to move in time to the music, anything seems possible. When we dance, we can be trees or flowers or birds, or kings and queens, or fairies or monsters or wizards or dragons... We can feel our bodies transforming: getting stronger, lighter on our feet, more supple, more graceful. We can leap into the air, we can twist and turn, we can let ourselves be swept along by the music and escape to a magic dancing kingdom. It's all so exciting!

Now, let me tell you about some of my ballet school friends...

Peter. There aren't many boys in our class, but Peter is one of them and he's good. He's mad about sport as well as ballet, especially football. Like me, he's not tall for his age – he's 10 – but he's got strong muscles. He likes to have his hair cut short in a really cool style. He says he can't see to dance if it's flopping over his face; I expect he's right. He'd be very embarrassed if he heard me saying this, but I think he's got beautiful brown eyes.

Gloria. She's about the same age as me, but she's much taller. I wish I had lovely long legs like her; they make her look so elegant when she dances. Unlike me, she doesn't fidget. She's got what they call 'poise'. Her hair is curly brown and styled in cornrow braids. She's kind and helpful – and she plays the piano beautifully!

Jessamy. I hate to admit this, but she's the best dancer in our class. Ever so much better than me! She started ballet late, when she was almost eight, so she's older than most of us in the class. But she's learning very fast and will soon overtake us, I think, and be moved up a class to study for the next grade. She's nearly 11 now, and is working hard at school. She finds it hard to do all her homework and her ballet practice, some days. She seems rather serious at first, but is good fun when you get to know her. She's slim and delicate-looking and has curly red hair that's hard to keep neat and tidy in proper ballet fashion.

Darcey. Darcey's the only pupil in our class who doesn't really want to be here. Her mum has always loved ballet, and hoped to have a daughter who'd be a dancer. So, as you can see, she named Darcey after the famous ballerina, and sent her to ballet lessons. But – here's the problem – Darcey prefers the outdoor life. She's crazy about animals. She still comes to classes for now because she likes to meet her friends. She says ballet exercises help her to keep fit. She's quite right. They do!

Chapter 1

Oh No!

Sid Johnson stood in the kitchen doorway, his mouth open in horror. As if to defend himself from attack, he clenched one hand into a tight fist. With the other, he steadied himself against the door frame. He was a strong man, tough and athletic, but if you looked closely, you could see that he was shaking.

But his wife was not looking. She had her back towards him as she sleepily filled the kettle, ready to make them both an early morning cup of tea.

'Sid! Shhh!' she said. 'Not so loud! The kids are still asleep upstairs. And do watch what you say! Willow's so quick to learn, these days. Those acting classes at ballet school are turning her into a right little copycat. It's all very clever, of course, but sometimes I do wonder... and, anyway, I don't want her using swear words!'

She switched the kettle on, turned round, and, at last, caught sight of her husband.

'Sid!' she cried in alarm, rushing over to him. She peered anxiously into his face. 'Sid! What on earth's the matter! Are you OK? Do you feel ill?'

'Look!' said Sid. He pointed through the open door and out into the backyard. 'Look!' he said again, hoarsely. 'Look! My bikes! They're gone!'

Apart from his wife and children, bikes were Sid Johnson's greatest interest in life. He cycled everywhere – to his work in the big solar panel factory, to the shops (especially the bike shop), to the library and the swimming pool, to the old Town Hall where they held great gigs on Saturday nights, to meet his cycling teammates, and to collect Willow and her younger brother

Jake from school. In the evenings he spent hours tinkering with his bikes; at weekends, he rode races on them. Usually, he kept them safely locked up in his backyard. But this morning, his bikes weren't there. They had disappeared!

Josie Johnson pulled the belt of her dressing gown tight around her waist, squeezed herself sideways past her husband – he seemed frozen to the spot – and stepped out through the doorway into the backyard. She was a calm, level-headed person, always good in a crisis – she was training to be a nurse, after all – but what she saw now set her own heart pounding. Missing bikes were only part of the problem.

'How could they!' she gasped. 'How could they?! What a horrible, horrible thing to do!'

19

Upstairs, Willow Johnson stirred uneasily in her sleep, perhaps disturbed by the commotion in the backyard below. Her dreams – of dancing, of course – faded away, and slowly, she opened her eyes. The light gleaming through the curtains told her that it was morning, but was it time to get up? Lazily, she stretched, then snuggled down again under the covers. 'No, don't go back to sleep,' she told herself; she really had better look at the time. She reached out to pick up the alarm clock. Aahhh... just twenty past six; she could spend a few more minutes in bed. Half-awake, half-asleep, she smiled as she remembered that today was Friday: Ballet School day!

For almost four years now, Willow had been going to classes at Rosewood Ballet School.... At first, just once a week, but now she went twice, on Tuesdays and Fridays. When Willow was working hard towards the official Grade exams, there were extra sessions on

Saturdays, too, and towards the end of term, there might be Sunday afternoon rehearsals for the performances that each class put on to entertain their families and friends.

'You know, sometimes I worry about so much ballet,' said Mrs Johnson to Willow's class teacher at primary school. 'I don't want it interfering with her school work…'

But Willow loved it all. She was a good dancer – light on her feet, full of energy and a quick learner; that is, when she paid attention. She loved performing. Her teachers said she was 'musical' – yes, she always kept in time to the beat, but there was much more than that to her dancing. She used her swift, graceful movements – and the expressions on her pale, wide-eyed little face – to show what the music was trying to say.

'In fact,' said Madame Olga, the principal of Rosewood Ballet School, in her thick Russian accent, 'I don't think Willow is a dancer!

Instead, she is an actor who can dance.'

Madame Olga was talking to Miss Sally Francisco, Willow's ballet class teacher, who nodded her head in agreement. Madame Olga continued: 'I don't see Willow's future as a ballerina. But acting and dancing on stage – or even in films – well, there, Willow might do well. *If* she works hard, of course, and if she has good luck. Right now, she should keep on with the ballet classes, I think. Ballet skills are the foundation for so many other kinds of dance. If Willow can do well at ballet, she can dance anything!'

'Also...' Madame Olga had glanced across the room to where Willow, hopping from one foot to another, and her friends were waiting for their lesson to start, '...learning the discipline of ballet will help her concentrate, and calm her down. She's never still, that little one!'

But this morning, Willow was still, for just a little while. She snuggled deeper under the covers, and gave a little contented sigh. At least ten more minutes in bed...

Her mind wandered back to yesterday after school, when she'd spent a lovely time with Samira, who lived next door. Every Thursday she went to Samira's house, because Mrs Johnson had to work late at the hospital. In their own way, thought Willow, Thursdays with Samira and her family were almost as much fun as going to the ballet school.

'I've spoken to Mrs Khan,' Willow's Mum had said at the beginning of the school term. 'It's all arranged. She'll collect you from school along with Samira. You'll go home with her and stay there until your father gets home from the factory. You and Samira can play – AND do your homework together – and Mrs Khan has very kindly said that she'll give you something to eat. Then, as soon as you're home, young lady, it's a bath and into your pyjamas and ready for bed. No messing! Understood? You can read in bed, or perhaps your Dad will read to you...'

'Huh,' Willow had interrupted, 'all he reads is books about bikes...'

'And all *you* read is books about ballet!' Mrs Johnson had replied.

'Now, here's a thought,' she'd continued, with a smile. 'Perhaps I should write books about a ballet-mad cyclist, or about dancing on two wheels... I might make my fortune! Or at least I might keep my family happy!'

'Mum! Per-leese...! It's not *funny*. Ballet is very, very important!' Willow sometimes had a bit of a sense of humour failure where ballet was concerned.

'Of course it is! I shouldn't joke about it!' Mrs Josie Johnson had smiled. Changing the subject, she'd gone on speaking, but quietly, as if she were talking to herself.

'We're all so fortunate, in this street, to have such good neighbours. Sometimes I don't know how we'd manage without them! Mrs Khan is so thoughtful, so helpful, especially now I'm studying so hard. And student nurses have to be on duty at such unusual hours.'

Suddenly her voice had became brisker, more commanding.

'Now – are you listening, Willow? – you must be on your very best behaviour whenever you go to Samira's house. No rushing wildly around, like you sometimes do at home. No shrieking or shouting. And remember to say "please" and "thank you"...'

Willow had pulled a face. 'Mum!' she had said, protesting. 'Samira's my friend. Of course I'll behave. I love going round to her house. Mrs Khan is nice, too, and so is little Jamil. He can walk now, and he's learning to talk. Samira's been helping him. And guess what?' Willow

beamed proudly. 'He can almost say my name –
he calls me Lo-Lo.'

That had been two weeks ago. This morning,
still snuggled cosily in her bed, Willow sleepily
recalled the conversation.

'Although Mum fusses about me,' she
thought, 'she really doesn't need to worry. It's
great going next door to see Samira and her
family.' Even though Samira didn't do and
wasn't interested in ballet, her and Willow
still had lots of fun together. They shared their
worries and secrets – and sometimes even their
clothes! – and they could always make each
other laugh. They would often help each other
with their schoolwork, sitting next to each other
in most of their lessons. Although sometimes
they would chatter too much and get moved by
teachers to opposite sides of the classroom.

Samira was much better than Willow at
drawing, IT and maths. She could also speak
three languages, which Willow thought was
really clever.

Sometimes, Willow would try to tell Samira
about the dances she was learning and show
her some of the ballet steps. Willow knew
that Samira wasn't really that interested, but
Samira understood how much dancing meant
to her friend and so she would always listen –
for a while, at least! Then Samira might tease
Willow about her dancing or change the subject.
Samira was always talking about a new
program on her laptop that helped her to create
designs on-screen.

Willow snuggled further under the bedcovers
and remembered sitting after school in
Samira's garden in the sunshine with Samira's
Mum and her baby brother, Jamil. For the
time of year, it was really warm; Mrs Khan had
filled an old bowl with water and Jamil had a

lovely time splashing about in it. Samira folded some paper to make a little boat that floated on the water – until it got soggy and sank – and Jamil loved that, too. Willow and Samira drank orange juice and ate some cake that Mrs Khan had made, together with a few rather squashy strawberries.

'Last of the season, from MY garden,' Samira had said, proudly.

Then, while Samira stretched out on the grass with her drawing book – she liked colouring really complicated patterns – Willow practised a few steps from the dance she was learning for her end of term performance.

Jamil bounced up and down on Mrs Khan's lap and watched; then he laughed and waved his arms as if he was trying to copy Willow.

Mrs Khan had turned their backyard into a really lovely garden. Samira had helped, too, after school and at the weekends.'You see, she has the green fingers,' Mrs Khan said to

Willow one day. 'And…' she said, taking her daughter's hand and peering at it, 'and also the dirty fingernails with garden earth underneath them! Go and wash your hands, please. Now!'

As well as proper soft, cushiony grass – which was great to dance on in bare feet – there were pink and white roses, and daffodils in springtime, and honeysuckle climbing up the house walls, and window-boxes with red geraniums and some white trailing flowers that Willow didn't know the name of. There was a little greenhouse, as well, with tomatoes and herbs and Samira's strawberries growing in pots, and, outside, there were rows of lettuces and carrots and green beans and lots and lots of spinach. There were big black plastic boxes full of earth where potatoes grew, and, beside the path, little clumps of marigolds and pansies and a blue flower with strange hairy leaves.

'It's all so much nicer than our backyard!' Willow thought to herself. 'That just has

cracked concrete and Dad's bikes and his
bike rack and old toolshed, and the rubbish
and recycling bins, which get pretty smelly
in summer. And, of course, there's the hutch
and run for Mr Big Ears, Jake's rabbit. There
are lots of weeds, a tumbledown old tree, and
horrid prickly blackberries. And, when it rains,
slimy slugs and snails come out and creep
around! Ugh!'

While Samira went on drawing in the late
afternoon sunshine, Willow had told her a bit
about the dances she was learning at Ballet
School this term. Miss Francisco – her teacher
– had worked out new steps for them, but
she had taken the idea for the dances from
a famous old ballet called *The Nutcracker*. It
featured a magic Kingdom of Sweets, ruled
over by the Sugar Plum Fairy, and so, in their
dances, they all pretended to be different
sweets or cakes. Willow was a chocolate button,
Gloria was a peppermint, Darcey was a toffee,

Olly was a marshmallow, Sophie and Molly were jelly babies, and Peter and Darren did a very funny dance together as chewing gum. Jessamy would be the Sugar Plum Fairy, in charge of them all, because she was the best dancer in their class.

'Pretending to be dancing sweets sounds very silly, but when you see the whole ballet – I've watched it on TV – it sort of makes sense, and some of the dances in it are totally awesome,' Willow had told Samira. 'The one I like best is the one where Russian dancers do amazing leaps and jumps, and the Sugar Plum Fairy's variation – her big solo – is great. It's one of the most difficult dances that any ballerina has to do. It's full of really complicated steps, and she ends up dancing round and round the stage in a series of *fouettés* – these really fast turns balancing on one leg. It's brilliant and scary, as she could easily fall over, and utterly exhausting!'

Even Willow's Dad had stopped what he was doing to watch that bit of the ballet on television.

'She's quite an athlete,' he said, pointing to the Fairy, and he was right!

Willow reminded herself to take the CD of the ballet music round to Samira's the following week. Willow thought she might like it, although the music was very, very old fashioned. Miss Francisco had told them that it was written by a Russian composer called Tchaikovsky, who lived over 100 years ago.

Willow smiled to herself, and remembered more about the afternoon in Samira's garden. While Samira was drawing, Mrs Khan had watched Willow dance, and listened – a bit – to her explaining the Nutcracker ballet story.

'It's all about a handsome prince who's been put under a spell by a magician and turned into an old-fashioned Nutcracker – a thing for getting nuts out of their shells, a bit

like the pliers my Dad uses for bike repairs,'
Willow had said. 'A girl called Clara is given
the Nutcracker at Christmas. It comes to life,
and so do some more Christmas presents: toy
soldiers. They all fight with giant mice – I don't
know where they come from – and then the
Nutcracker turns back into a prince and takes
Clara through a snowstorm – there are lovely
snowflake dances – to meet the Sugar Plum
Fairy in the Kingdom of the Sweets. There,
Clara watches while all the different sweets
do show-off dances, then the Sugar Plum
Fairy and her partner, Prince Coughdrop (yes,
really!), do solos and a grand pas-de-deux to
entertain them.'

'That does not sound to me like a very
healthy ballet!' Mrs Khan had said. 'Too many
sweets! You should be the dancing flowers
instead – that would be pretty! Or the dancing
fruits... They are pretty, too. And much better
for you...'

Samira had stopped drawing and started to giggle. 'Ooh Mum!' she said, rolling over on the grass. 'Willow couldn't do that! Whoever heard of The Dance of the Squashy Strawberries?!'

Willow pulled the covers tight around herself, and laughed again at the memory.

Chapter 2
A Horrible Shock

'Jake! Jake?! Willow! Willow?!'

Mrs Johnson's voice echoed sharply up the stairs. 'Are you awake? It's time to get up! But don't come downstairs just yet, please. I'm on my way to see you both, right now.'

Willow sat bolt upright in bed. This was very strange! Usually, every morning, their mother called them to hurry and get dressed and come downstairs to have breakfast. But not today. Why not? What was going on?

Willow heard footsteps approaching, and in just a few moments her mother's clever, kindly face peered round the bedroom door. She looked rather worried.

Yawning, and still in his pyjamas, Jake padded in from the room next to Willow. He flung himself down on to Willow's bed rather more energetically than was strictly necessary, sprawling across both her feet.

'Owwww!' said Willow. 'Get OFFFFF! Don't do that! You mustn't hurt my feet! I need them to be strong and healthy for dancing...'

'Sit still, Jake,' said Mrs Johnson. She caught sight of Willow's anxious expression, and tried to smile.

'Don't worry, Willow love, everything's fine. But something rather bad has happened, and I need to tell you about it.'

Downstairs, Willow heard her father, talking on his mobile phone.

'Hello? Hello?! Is that the police station?'

'No, we don't know who did it.'

Mrs Johnson was perched on the corner of Willow's bed; Jake was cuddled up beside her, for once quiet and still instead of noisy and boisterous and bouncy. Willow had bundled herself up in the bed covers; even so, she felt cold and shivery.

'What seems to have happened,' Mrs Johnson continued, 'is that someone broke into our backyard last night. They stole all your father's bikes – that's bad enough – but they've also left a horrible mess behind them. It was done deliberately, as if they wanted to cause as much damage and upset as possible. They smashed their way into the toolshed, then knocked over the bins and scattered rubbish all around. They found some old tins of paint in the shed, and they've poured that over the concrete. Then they tried – very quietly, it must have been – to climb in through the back room window. But all they managed to do was break the glass...'

Willow stretched out her hand to pick up her tablet from the bedside table. It was full of all her favourite ballet videos and music. She hugged it tightly to her.

Mrs Johnson sighed, and read the question in Willow's frightened face.

'Yes, I think that does mean that they wanted to see what they could find to steal inside the house. There's broken glass all over the back room carpet – that's why you must stay upstairs for the moment. But I don't think they meant to harm us. Just property… not men or women or children. Some bad – or ill – people just seem to take pleasure in thieving and destroying; I don't know why.'

'Now, let's look on the bright side,' said Mrs Johnson, trying to sound cheerful. 'No one's hurt, and no one did break in, after all. Your father's called the police, and I don't think we should touch anything until they arrive. But after they've seen and photographed all they need, we can get going with cleaning and clearing up. We'll soon have the house – and backyard – back to normal.'

Willow found that she could not stop the tears trickling down her cheeks.

'Oh Willow, love, don't cry!' said her mum. 'It will be all right, you'll see. It's just a horrible shock for us all, and of course your father is furious – as well as very, very upset – about his bikes being stolen. But they were insured, so he'll be able to buy new ones.'

She smiled, sadly this time, and shook her head.

'But they won't be the ones he's cared for so lovingly over all these years... We'll just have to be extra nice and kind to him, to help him get over it.'

She sighed. 'We'll manage. We'll come though this. I'm absolutely certain. But...'

'Mum, Muuuummm!!' Jake's voice rose in a sudden wail that startled both Willow and their mother. 'What about Mr Big Ears? Is he safe? I want to see him!'

'Not just now, Jake,' Mrs Johnson's voice was gentle but very determined. 'I expect he's there somewhere, but he's not in his hutch at the moment. The intruders kicked that over, as well...'

Jake flung himself into her arms, sobbing as if his heart would break.

'There, there...' said Mrs Johnson, 'we'll do our very best to find him. You know how timid he is; he probably hasn't gone far. And your spiders are OK. Their box is undamaged. They probably didn't see it in the dark.'

She shuddered slightly. Jake's pet spiders were not her favourites. They were housed in a plastic vivarium – a fancy old name for a box where creatures lived. And that was kept in the shed in the yard, NOT in the house!

Willow put her arms around her little brother. A horrible thought came into her mind,

though she cared too much for Jake's feelings
to speak it out loud. What if the people who'd
stolen Dad's bikes had stolen Mr Big Ears, too?
She knew that some people *ate* rabbits!

At last Jake stopped crying. Mrs Johnson got
up off the bed and helped him to stand, rather
shakily, beside her.

'Now I want you both to be brave,' she said.
'Go and get dressed. Put on something warm –
Willow, you're shivering! – then wait upstairs
for me. I'm going to get you some breakfast –
you'll feel better if you eat something – and I'm
going to phone Ruby. I think she has this week
off from her work at the Beauty Salon; she told
me the other day when she collected Gloria
from ballet school that she was hoping to make
a start on the costumes for your end of term
performance. If she's free, I'll ask her whether

she can look after you this morning.'

Ruby was Gloria's grown-up sister. She was fascinated by stage clothes and make-up, and knew loads about them. She often made or mended costumes and helped Ballet School pupils get ready for their performances. As Miss Francisco said backstage before one particularly complicated little ballet, 'Where we'd be without you, Ruby, I really don't know!'

Mrs Johnson felt rather the same today. She went on talking to Jake and Willow:

'Neither of you is in a fit state for school – at least, not until lunchtime. I'll need to be downstairs, talking to the police and then helping your dad to clear up indoors and in the backyard. That's no place for children at the moment! Then I'm on duty in the hospital at two o'clock. Even trainee nurses – especially trainee nurses – can't let their patients down!'

Brrrrriiinnnnnggggg!

'That's the doorbell.' Mrs Johnson peered

through the bedroom window into the street at the front of the house.

'Ah! A police car, and two officers. Your dad will let them in...'

As she went downstairs, the comforting smile left Mrs Johnson's face and was replaced by an anxious frown.

'Well,' she said to herself, 'I've told them what's happened here. But how will they feel when they learn what's been done next door?'

She rang Ruby's number. 'Oh no! That's terrible!' said Ruby. 'How can anyone be so cruel?! Of course I can help. Don't worry; I'll be round straight away.'

Mrs Johnson heard her husband talking to the policeman and policewoman in the back yard. 'I kept the bikes here, in this rack,' he said. 'Yes, they were always locked. And there was a waterproof cover – like a metal shell – that was locked on top of them...'

Mrs Johnson made her way towards the

sound of the voices.

Brrrrriiinnnnngggggg!

It was the bell, again. Mrs Johnson turned back, and hurried to open the front door. On the step, she found Mrs Khan and baby Jamil, and Willow's best friend, Samira. All three of them were crying.

'Oh Josie!' Mrs Khan sobbed. 'Josie! Have you seen...? I can't believe...Why? Why? My beautiful garden...!'

'My dear! Please, please come in!' Mrs Johnson said, putting her arm round Mrs Khan's shoulders and leading her gently into the kitchen. 'Come through this way – we can't go into the back room until the police have examined it. I don't think there's any broken glass in here, but watch where you tread, all the same...'

She helped Mrs Khan sink down into the battered old armchair that stood in the corner of the kitchen. Jamil sat on his mother's lap, while Samira perched on one of the arms of the chair, as close as she could to both of them.

Mrs Johnson crouched down beside the chair, and handed Mrs Khan a box of tissues.

'Oh, isn't it awful?' she said, shaking her head. 'Unbelievable! How can anyone do a thing like this? In our nice friendly street...'

'Is Mr Khan still at work?' asked Mrs Johnson. Mrs Khan nodded. 'So he doesn't know...?'

Mr Khan was an ambulance driver who worked at the big hospital where Josie Johnson was doing her nurse training. Often, he worked night shifts. This morning, he had not yet got home.

'I tried to phone him,' said Mrs Khan, 'but he was out on a call. They took a message, and said they'd tell him. He's due home soon, anyway. But what if he hasn't got the message and comes home to find a police car outside the house? It will be a terrible shock for him...'

She sniffed and frowned. Then, looking down at Samira, she tried to smile.

'Come on, Samira, sweetheart,' she said. 'No more tears. We're safe here. Let's dry those eyes.'

'Knock, knock!' There was a soft tapping at the kitchen door. 'It's only me!' called Ruby. 'The front door was open. Can I come in?'

'Hello Mrs Khan! Hello Samira! Hello little Jamil,' Ruby said, smiling kindly, but sadly, at them all. 'I'm so very, very sorry to hear what happened. Now, is there anything I can do to help? Would anyone like a cup of tea?'

Josie Johnson stayed talking quietly to Mrs Khan and Samira, while Ruby made tea, put bread in the toaster and poured milk and cereal into bowls for Willow and Jake. She offered some to Samira, as well, but Samira shook her head and turned her face away.

'That's all right,' said Ruby, softly. 'Breakfast can wait. But let's leave the grown-ups to talk to the police, just for a little while. Do you think you could be a kind, helpful girl and take this toast upstairs to Willow? I know she'd love to see you – and I expect she's very hungry.'

She held out a gentle hand toward Samira, who didn't say anything but got up and walked past her, out of the kitchen and up the stairs to Willow's room. Ruby followed, with the cereal and the toast.

Another friendly face peered round the door. It was Kirsty MacTavish, from three houses down the street.

'Och, Mrs Khan, hen!' she exclaimed. 'How are you? And how are the wee ones? Your poor garden! All the plants pulled up and the greenhouse in ruins. What a terrible, terrible thing to happen! In our nice friendly street! What monsters the people who did it must be!'

She turned towards Willow's dad, who had just walked into the kitchen. A woman in police uniform was close behind him.

'They took your bikes, as well, I hear?' Kirsty continued, shaking her head. 'Och! Tsk, tsk! You'll be lost without them, for sure!' She was a very clever woman – a computer programmer for a big city bank – but once she started talking it was almost impossible to stop her.

'Tsk! That's bad; very, very bad. You know that someone has broken down my fence, and tried to get in through the glass doors in my dining room? AND...' Kirsty paused for breath, '...I hear that Terry Simmonds has had his bike stolen, too, and his satellite dish pulled right off the wall. AND Sadie Watson from number 27 phoned me just now, and said that they were disturbed in the night by their dog barking. They went down to see whether anything was the matter – it's a bonny beast, but awful nervous. But – so Sadie said – it quietened down when it saw them, so they went back to bed and didn't think any more about it, until they went out into their garden this morning and saw our broken fence AND red paint – just like blood! – sprayed all over their back wall. AND old Mrs Watson's back gate has been ripped off its hinges, AND Mr Patel from the corner shop says that his fence is broken too, AND his big rubbish bins have been emptied all over the main road – what a mess! – AND, what's so much, much worse, his delivery van has been daubed with awful words. I won't say them now...'

She caught sight of Mrs Khan's anguished face.

'Och, nooo!' she cried in horror. 'Not you, too?!' Mrs Khan nodded and, very quietly, started to cry once more.

'I haven't told Samira and I don't want her to know,' she sniffed. 'As soon as the police have seen the words, I will cover them up with fresh paint or something. Then...' Mrs Khan suddenly sat up straight and pushed up the long sleeves of her cardigan. Her brown eyes flashed and a determined look settled on her face. 'And then...and then...I'll make a new garden for Samira!'

Chapter 3

Back to Normal?

uby was quite right. In spite of the shock, Willow and Jake were hungry. But the moment Willow caught sight of Samira's tear-stained face, all thoughts of breakfast vanished – for the moment – from her mind.

'Oh!' she gasped, 'oh Samiiiiraaa!' She rushed across the room and put one arm around her friend's shoulder. She helped Samira walk, rather shakily, across the room and the two friends sat side by side on Willow's bed, holding hands but saying nothing. After a few minutes, Willow found Aurora, her old, shabby, dearly-loved ballet dancer rag doll, and silently handed it to Samira to cuddle.

Ruby perched on the little chair by the desk where Willow often did her homework. 'Eat up, Jake!' she said. 'And while you're eating, I'll tell you a story. About brave sailors, bold explorers, buried treasure and a magic princess who lived on the Caribbean island where my grandmother was born.'

It was a good story, and Ruby was an excellent storyteller. Slowly, Willow and Samira found themselves listening, and then humming along with the sailors' shanty that Ruby was teaching Jake to sing. By the time Ruby's explorers had met the princess and found the fabulous treasure, Willow felt well enough to eat her cereal, and even Samira managed to nibble a tiny square of toast and jam. From downstairs, they heard the noise of the front door opening and closing, over and over again, and loud grown-up voices, then the thump and swish of a heavy broom and the roaring wail of the vacuum cleaner.

Jake peered out of the bedroom window. 'The police car's gone,' he said. 'What's going to happen now?'

Quick, light footsteps sounded outside the bedroom door. It was Willow's mum, with a plate of sandwiches, a few little tomatoes, a packet of biscuits, a big bottle of juice, and a red net bag full of tangerines.

'Here we are! A picnic for lunch!' she said, with a rather harassed smile. 'I've got to go to work soon and so has your Dad.'

She turned to talk to Ruby. 'Is it still OK for you to stay here and give these three their lunch, then drive them to school in time for afternoon lessons?'

Ruby nodded. 'No problem!' she said, cheerfully.

'Fantastic!' said Willow's mum. 'You don't know how helpful that is! Ruby, you are a STAR!'

'And Jake, I've got some fantastic news for you. We've found Mr Big Ears and he's safe and well! He was hiding behind one of the rubbish bins. He's a bit dirty and very frightened, but otherwise he's fine. We've put him in a cardboard box in the kitchen with some cabbage leaves to nibble. Come downstairs with me, just for a moment, and you can see him now. Then, this weekend, you can help Dad to make him a nice new hutch and run.'

Jake gave a whoop of delight – and burst into tears again.

Mrs Johnston walked across the room and stood beside Willow's bed.

'Samira, dear, your mother will meet you at the school gate as usual after lessons end this afternoon. And Willow – are you paying attention? – Peter's mum will take you and Peter to the ballet school straight from ordinary school, then Dad will collect you and bring you both home. Be good! Take care! I love you!'

As Mrs Johnston hurried out of the room, Willow felt a sudden pang of alarm, almost as if her brother Jake had leapt out from behind a door to surprise her – one of his favourite, really annoying, tricks. For the first time in her life she had forgotten that today was Friday, the day she always went to Rosewood Ballet School. Thank goodness her mum had remembered!

Hurriedly, she found her ballet bag and checked that everything was ready inside it. Leotard? Yes! Short pink socks? Yes! Cardigan? Yes! Notebook? Pencil? Yes, they were there! Hairbrush, hairband, hairnet, hairpins? Yes, yes, yes, yes! But something was missing, Willow felt sure. What could it be? Oh no, surely not! The absolute essential – how could she forget them? Her favourite pale pink leather ballet shoes!

'And TWO and THREE and FOUR! Keep that leg straight... and toes pointed! Don't twist those hips!'

Miss Sally Francisco's clear, high voice rang out round the dance studio. Along with the rest of her class, Willow was standing at the barre, doing the familiar warm-up exercises that began every dance lesson and rehearsal.

'Very nice, Darcey,' trilled Miss Francisco. 'But watch those heels as you bend your knees. Keep them low. And feet in SECOND position, remember! Keep control, Peter, keep control! Lift that arm gracefully and with purpose, don't just swing it around.'

Earlier that afternoon, Willow had found ordinary school surprisingly difficult. They'd been reading and writing poems about autumn, and so many had mentioned trees and leaves or fruits and flowers. Each one reminded Willow of Mrs Khan's vandalised garden, and she'd felt really worried that they might upset Samira. But Samira just sat quietly next to her at their classroom table, not speaking at all, as if she was lost in a dream.

As she drove them to school, Ruby had spoken kindly to them. 'Yes, we've all had a shock,' she had said, 'but at school you'll be in safe, familiar surroundings, and with all your friends. Of course you want to help clear up all the mess, and I'm sure you can. But there's nothing you can do at home right now, and you don't want to miss any lessons.'

That had sounded sensible, but, looking at Samira, Willow wondered if Ruby had been right. As they put on their coats, ready to go home, she stood very close to her friend and whispered, 'Are you OK?'

Samira had managed a faint smile and a whispered 'Yes' in return. But even so, Willow was still worried.

Now, however, as Willow followed the familiar routine at Rosewood Ballet School, she did at last feel safe once more. As her legs bent and stretched and her toes tapped and pointed, life began to seem normal again. She even dared hope that everything could be put right, in her own home and her neighbours' houses. The broken glass could be swept up; the spilled paint could be washed away; the trampled fences could be repaired or rebuilt. Her father could buy new bikes – in some ways, he'd like that! But what about Samira's garden? That would take years of hard work and loving care for Mrs Khan to recreate, even with help from Samira. 'I will help too,' promised Willow.

'Jessamy, keep your shoulders turned this way, to the front,' called Miss Francisco. 'Good, Sophie. A nice clean movement. Let's see that *relevé* again! Begin with *plié* in third position. Straighten your knees, move one foot behind the other and lift both heels off the floor to *demi-pointe*. Raise one knee so that your front foot comes up to touch the front of your knee. Keep those toes pointed! That's it! Well done! Now, straighten your leg so that you're balancing with both feet at *demi-pointe* again, give a little jump to move them apart – third position – then bend both knees back to *demi-plié* and you're ready to do your next step.'

Miss Francisco walked across the studio floor, watching carefully as her class moved

Relevé

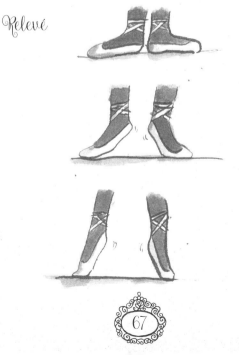

Plié

in time to the lively music from Mrs Chang's piano. She was pleased. They were all working hard this term, and making good progress. Some were better dancers than others, of course; that was only to be expected. However – and here was a surprise – this afternoon, for the first time, she was beginning to have a few worries about Willow.

Willow of all people! Willow had talent and was very keen; one of her more promising pupils. But today – well, Miss Francisco's years of experience as a teacher told her that something was not quite right with Willow's dancing.

'Willow! Concentrate, please!' she called. 'I don't know what you're thinking about, but is your mind really on your dancing? Your exercises are technically quite good, but there's no feeling for the music. I don't know why, but you're dancing like a machine today, and I don't like it.'

Miss Francisco continued, 'I'm going to snap my fingers and bring back my lovely, lively, expressive little Willow. Are you ready? Take a deep breath, and let's begin the last set of *développés* again. One, two, three..!'

For the rest of the warm-up, Willow danced well. Miss Francisco was right, she had not been concentrating. But now she had to! In just a few minutes, they were going to rehearse their end of term solos, one by one, in front of the whole class. Everyone felt nervous, though they tried not to show it.

Miss Francisco clapped her hands. 'Listen, everyone!' she commanded. 'Take a quick breather – just a couple of minutes. I've got some important news to announce. This Christmas, Rosewood Ballet School is planning to take a group of pupils to the Grand Theatre to see a live performance of *The Nutcracker*. As you know, Christmas is the traditional time to perform the ballet, since it features magical Christmas presents and a huge Christmas tree. Seeing the ballet should be a great experience: Carlos Kasparov is dancing the Prince, and Samantha Jerez-Martini will be the Sugar Plum Fairy. They both have very strong technique and are excellent dramatic dancers. We can learn a lot by watching them. I'll be handing out letters about this trip at the end of class. Madame Olga has managed to arrange special cheap tickets for ballet students, so I hope that many of you will be able to come.'

'Oooh – how exciting! I wish I could go!' thought Willow. But she didn't think her mum and dad would be able to afford it. She'd seen *The Nutcracker* on screen, but a real live performance with world-famous dancers in front of her on stage would be so much more thrilling. She wondered if Kasparov was really as handsome as he looked in photos.

Miss Francisco clapped her hands again. 'Now – who's first in our own rehearsal? Where are our jelly babies? Ah – come along, Sophie and Molly!'

One by one, and in pairs, the class rehearsed their dances.

By the time the class ended, Willow felt exhausted. It was not just the dancing – though her solo as a chocolate button, rolling and bouncing across the floor, was full of very energetic hops and skips and bounces. No, she felt tired in her mind and spirit, as well as in her body; it had been a strange and stressful day.

After she and all her classmates had made the traditional *révérence* to Miss Francisco, bowing and curtseying in graceful ballet style to show their respect for their teacher, Willow hurried off to the changing rooms. She felt chilly now that she'd stopped dancing. She just wanted to pull on her warm hoody sweatshirt and leggings, wrap her soft padded coat around her, and go home.

Révérence

But the other girls had heard about the overnight attack on the street where Willow lived, and wanted to ask her all about it. They weren't being nosy – they were worried and concerned. And, like everyone else, they were shocked that something so violent could happen in quiet, ordinary, unremarkable streets in the city where they lived. If Willow's house had been attacked, were their own homes safe, they wondered?

'Did they really break your windows?' asked Molly.

'Your Dad must be so upset about his bikes!' said Sophie.

'How dreadful, having to clear up all that mess!' cried Jess. 'And poor Mr Patel at the shop! How will he manage without a van to fetch and carry milk and bread and newspapers?'

Gloria joined in. She had already heard something from Ruby, her big sister.

'It's dreadful that so many houses were attacked! What did the police say? Do they know who did it?'

Animal lover Darcey thought about people's pets, of course. 'That dog must have been terrified when it heard the attacker!' she said. 'And – oh my, I've only just remembered! – what about Jake's rabbit, and his spiders?'

Willow slumped down on one of the changing room benches and leaned back against some rather scratchy wool coats hanging from hooks on the wall. She let all the questions fly around her. She gave a weary sigh, and tried to tell her ballet friends all she knew. Which wasn't very much, really. Like Samira, she hadn't seen the bad words on the wall – Mrs Khan had covered them up before the friends were allowed out of the back door on their way to school in the afternoon. So all she really knew about were the thefts and the damage – and the reassuring fact that no one had been hurt. But, even so, she could not forget the sight of Samira's ruined garden, with plants ripped from the ground, rose bushes torn and trampled, flowerpots kicked over and the remains of the greenhouse in a sad and crumpled heap in a corner.

'No, they don't know who did it,' she said. 'But Mr Big Ears is safe. And the spiders, worse luck. I think the dog is OK, as well. But, but,' and she couldn't stop a sob rising in her throat, or her voice shaking, 'it's Samira's garden – it's terrible! It's ruined...'

She could not go on. Pictures of the mess and damage and heaps of dying flowers flashed back into her mind. Would they stay there for ever?

Before Willow could say any more, Miss Francisco opened the changing room door. 'Still here, everyone?' she said in surprise. 'Come on! It's time to go home. And Willow – your father is outside in the hall. Hurry up, please! Don't keep him waiting!'

Willow grabbed her ballet bag and ran.

Chapter 4

Helping Hand

'Owww!' Jake dropped the hammer and put his fingers to his mouth, sucking them to try to ease the pain. It really was quite bad.

'Careful!' said his dad. 'What have you done!? Let's have a look...'

Gently, he took Jake's hand between his own rough, oil-stained fingers, and peered at it anxiously. 'That's OK,' he said with a sigh of relief. 'Let's go indoors and find a bag of peas from the freezer. We'll wrap that in an old towel, and rest your hand on it for a while. Then you'd better just sit quietly and watch me finish Mr Big Ears' new run. Later, you can help by passing the bits of wood that I need for the fence — but NOT by trying to knock nails in while my back is turned and bashing yourself with the hammer!'

It was Saturday morning, so there was no school. Jake and Sid Johnson were busy in the backyard, but Willow was still in the kitchen, doing nothing very much while her mum was sitting at the table, trying to check over some lecture notes on her laptop. Later, in the afternoon, Willow had one of her new acting classes at the Ballet School, but right now, the morning stretched ahead, dull and empty.

Willow felt bored and unsettled – and, if she were honest, still rather scared. Although she could not see it from the kitchen window, she knew that Samira's ruined garden was close by, just the other side of the fence that Dad was mending. She could not help worrying about her friend.

'Mum,' she said. 'Can I go round to Samira's?

I want to make sure she's OK.'

'Well, really, I don't know,' said Mrs Johnson. 'Do you have any homework this weekend? Have you put yesterday's ballet clothes in the dirty washing basket, and found a clean T-shirt and leggings to wear for your acting class this afternoon? Is your bedroom tidy? And what about a bit of practice on your recorder? You've hardly touched that all week!'

'Oh Mum, that's all so boring!' said Willow. 'My ballet bag is already packed and I'll do my homework tomorrow. There's not much. I promise! Pleeease...'

For a moment, in her eagerness to see Samira, Willow felt more like her usual self. So she stood up, tapped her mother on the shoulder, pointed to herself – in ballet mime, that meant 'Look at me' – and gave a huge, exaggerated yawn. Next, she made the ballet gestures that mean 'I am sad', looking down miserably at the floor, and running her fingers down her cheeks as if tears were falling. She followed this by the mime for 'I beg you', clasping her hands together close to her chest and then holding them out in front of her, reaching towards her mother. Finally, she gave another enormous false yawn, then slumped down at the kitchen table, rested her head on her folded arms, and pretended to go to sleep.

Willow's mum laughed. 'OK! OK! I get the message. Your acting's improving after just a few lessons! I'll ring and ask Mrs Khan whether it's convenient for you to go round. Now, where did I put my phone?'

While Mrs Johnson tapped in the number for Mrs Khan, Willow ran upstairs to her room to look for one of the ballet books she'd borrowed from the library. It told the stories of several famous ballets – including *The Nutcracker* – and had lots of photos of real live performances. She wanted to show it to Samira; she hoped she might like the designs for the colourful costumes and the stage scenery.

When she came downstairs again, her mum was looking rather serious.

'I'm sorry, Willow love,' she said, 'but you can't go round to Samira's house just now. Mrs Khan says that she's still in bed and fast asleep. She wants her to rest as much as possible today, because last night she kept being woken up by nightmares.'

'Now, get your recorder and your music book, and I'll help you learn a new tune. You can play it to Samira as soon as she feels better.'

Willow tried, but she really didn't feel like playing, and her hands moved awkwardly up and down the recorder, all clumsy fingers and thumbs.

'I can't *do* this,' she said fretfully. 'I'm *no good*. But I've got to learn music if I'm going to be a ballerina. I've really got to...' Suddenly, she felt as if she was going to cry. Angrily, she brushed the tears away with the back of her hand.

'Don't worry, Willow,' said her mum. 'It will
be all right. One day, you'll get the hang of it,
believe me! I expect you're still a bit shaken
after all yesterday's upheavals. Let's find a nice
DVD and you can curl up on the sofa and rest –
like Samira – until lunchtime.'

She searched through the untidy pile of discs
behind the television set. 'Look,' she said with
a smile. 'Here's something sweet and simple.
You used to love watching this when you were
tiny. I think it's one of the stories that made
you want to learn ballet in the first place!' And
she handed Willow a pink sparkly box covered
with pictures of a little ballet-dancing mouse in
a pretty frilly tutu.

The time out on the sofa definitely helped,
and later that afternoon, back again at

Rosewood Ballet School, Willow was thoroughly enjoying herself. There were no ballet grade exam classes this term; instead, Madame Olga had arranged a short course of lessons called 'Acting for the Ballet'. She had taught the first few classes herself – even in old age, she was very good, very strict and very terrifying. But from today, she had hired a new teacher to assist her, Monsieur Philippe Picot. He turned out to be young – and French – and really keen. He was small and slight, like Willow herself, and very light on his feet; all his movements were quick and nimble. He had a big nose, a wide smile and long hair tied back in a ponytail. Last year, he had worked for several months as a dancer in a big musical at the best theatre in the city, but right now he was 'resting'.

Willow's dad had explained that this meant that Monsieur Philippe didn't have a regular job in a theatre, but was trying to find work when and where he could.

'It's tough being an actor or a dancer or musician,' Dad had said. 'There are so many talented, well-trained people and not enough full-time jobs to go round. If they're lucky, they get taken on by a big company or an orchestra – sometimes, they're offered a contract that runs for years. But all too often, they are hired for just one season, or maybe only for a few performances. If they can teach, like your Monsieur Philippe, then that's a very useful way of earning enough money to live on.'

Willow had felt sorry that Monsieur Philippe couldn't find a theatre job, but pleased that he had come to Rosewood Ballet School. From the very first moment, she liked him.

The acting lessons began with simple breathing exercises. 'They're not like ballet movements,' Madame Olga had explained, 'but they're just as important. So, nice and relaxed, everyone! Stand easy – look straight ahead, keep your stomach in and make your spine tall, but let those shoulders drop down. Hold your hands loosely by your side, keep your feet a little way apart... Now, breathe iiiiin and ouuut, iiiiin and ouuut. Lovely! And again... Well done! Now raise your arms above your head, rise up *en relevé*, and down again. And up and stretch, and up and stretch...'

The exercises over, Madame Olga tottered back to her chair – she walked with a stick, these days – and sat down, with a sigh of relief.

'Now, Monsieur Philippe, I hand over to you,' said Madame Olga. 'I think you have things to say to the class...'

The new young teacher opened his arms wide – Ah! That means "Welcome", thought Willow – and beamed at the class.

'It's good to be here,' he began. 'I'm very pleased to meet you. I'm sorry that I don't yet know your names, but I hope I will soon learn them, and that we will have good fun practising our acting together. Perhaps you know this already,' he went on, 'but even if you do, it's worth saying again.' He took a deep breath and spoke extra slowly and clearly. 'Acting for ballet is special. It's not the same as acting in plays on stage. In particular, there's one very, very big difference. Can anyone tell me what it is?'

A tall girl called Ruth, standing at the back of the studio, put up her hand. Shyly, she asked, 'Is it because we don't use words in ballet?'

Monsieur Philippe gave the class another friendly smile. 'Yes! That's right,' he said. 'Exactly so! All the acting in ballet is done with movements – of the head, of the face, of the eyes, of the hands – in fact, we use the whole body to tell the audience what we are thinking or feeling. We don't need any words at all to communicate. But what we do need is *passion*.'

Monsieur Philippe patted his chest, above his heart, to give extra force to what he was saying.

'Unless we really believe in the character we

are acting and dancing, no one else will believe in it, either. So we must act, like we dance, with heart and soul and body!'

'Wow!' said Willow to herself. 'That's a lot to think about!'

'Let's try a little test,' said Monsieur Philippe. 'Look at me, and tell me what I am saying without words. See if you can understand – not what I am doing, but what I am feeling deep inside. Then you can try it yourselves.'

Monsieur Philippe stood straight and steady, then suddenly sprang upwards, tilting his weight on to his front leg. His other leg was slightly raised behind, as if he was ready to push off from his back foot and run away, very quickly. He lifted both his arms to above shoulder height, keeping the palms of his hands pointing towards the class – his audience. He held one hand firmly in front of his face, as if to shield it from danger. He raised the other hand high above his head, ready to fend off an attacker or push them away – though if you looked closely, you could also see that his fingertips were trembling. He opened his eyes wide, and parted his lips just a little, as if he were panting for breath. He held the pose for a few seconds, then relaxed with a smile.

'There! Did you understand?' asked Monsieur Philippe. 'Tell me – what was I miming?'

There was a little pause before the class found the courage to speak.'You were frightened,' several pupils then said at once. 'You were miming fear!'

'Exactly right!' beamed Monsieur Philippe. 'Now you try the same mime. We'll do it all together at first, practising one movement at a time. Then we'll put everything together, and see just how good you can all be!'

Some of the pupils, used to the strict routines of ballet class, began to giggle as they tried to pull frightened faces, or hold their hands high in the air. But a stern look from Madame Olga soon stopped that. After a few minutes, everyone was working well together.

Fear

Ruth, the tall girl at the back of the class, turned out to be really good at mime. Her gestures were crisp and elegant; her usually serious face came wonderfully alive with dramatic expressions. Michael, the boy who stood next to her, was bold and strong...

'That's a good start, both of you,' said
Monsieur Philippe. 'Be clear and simple, and
your audience will understand. Remember, in
a theatre, they are sitting a long way away.
Perhaps 50 metres from the stage or even
more. So every movement has to be slow and
deliberate – otherwise they might miss it. It
also has to be larger than life – but not silly
or exaggerated, otherwise the audience will
laugh at you, and not take you seriously, and
that would be a disaster! Above all – everyone
– remember all the time that you are dancers,
beautiful dancers! So keep all your movements
graceful, flowing, elegant...'

Almost without thinking, Willow raised
her arms in one of the gestures they'd been
practising, as smoothly and as gracefully as she
could. She fluttered her fingertips just a little
– then quickly dropped her hands to her sides,
suddenly realising what she was doing.

'Sorry,' she muttered, embarrassed. She

didn't know many of the pupils who came
to the Saturday acting class. Most of them
seemed friendly, but even so, she didn't want
to make a fool of herself in front of strangers.
It would have been different if her ballet class
friends had been there, but they were busy on
Saturdays with other things they liked to do.
Peter went to play football for the school, of
course, or – on special occasions – to watch the
local top league team at their home ground.
Darcey liked to be out in the open air, taking
her dog for long walks or watching birds in the
local wildlife park. Sometimes she helped out
at the City Farm, feeding the chickens and the
friendly little ponies. Gloria spent time with
her big, cheerful family, or learning new songs
with friends from her church choir. Jessamy
had homework – lots of it – and her Mum was
very strict about making her take a break from
dancing at weekends.

Feeling silly would not matter so much in

front of these familiar ballet friends, Willow thought. She was looking forward to seeing them again on Tuesday, at the next lesson. Miss Francisco had said they would use some of the class time to rehearse their group dances for the end of term performance.

But Monsieur Philippe was smiling again, and at her. 'No! Do not worry! That was nice, very nice,' he said. 'Like a little frightened bird. You are learning well. But now, please, you will stand still and listen. I have one more thing to say, before we all go home. Most important of all, of course, is that we have to perform our mime in time to the music. And – this is where it gets really clever – sometimes we have to mime at the same time as we are dancing! Has anyone seen the ballet called Swan Lake?'

Willow nodded; she had watched a DVD of it several times.

Monsieur Philippe was still speaking. 'Swan Lake has a famous scene where a Prince, hunting in the forest, meets a beautiful swan – and she explains to him in mime that she is really a young woman who has been transformed into a bird by an evil spell. She has to explain to him that if a handsome prince promises to love her, she will turn back into a human shape and they'll live happily ever after!'

Love

Olly and Darren sniggered. Monsieur Philippe laughed, too.

'Yes, said like that it does sound most unlikely, but good dancers – and great music – will make you believe that it's all real and important. It's not easy, but they can do it! I will bring the DVD next week to show you. And I will do the same mime myself. Then it will be your turn to try to act out a story to music. We can all practise being swans.'

As she got changed after the acting class, ready to go home, Willow realised that she had not thought about the attack on their street for most of the afternoon. Perhaps her Mum was right; she would soon feel better.

But what about Samira?

Chapter 5

All Together

'Hurry up, girls! Or we'll be late! We're walking to school – remember?!'

Sid Johnson was getting impatient. He had a busy morning ahead. First, he had to make sure that Willow, Jake – and Samira (thank goodness, she seemed OK) – got to school safely. Next, he had to call at the police station, to hand in a few old photos of his stolen bikes. He had little hope of ever seeing the bikes again, but the police had said that any evidence would be useful, and so he'd found the photos over the weekend. After that, he had to do some shopping – he was cooking supper tonight, while his wife was working at the hospital. And then, only then, could he get to his job at the factory. He'd have to arrange to work late for a few nights at the end of the week to make up the lost time.

'Come on Willow! Come on, Samira! What are you two doing up there?' Sid shouted upstairs towards Willow's bedroom, sighed heavily, but then smiled. This messing about was annoying, but it was good to see Samira and Willow together again.

There was a scurry of feet in the hallway, and the two girls rushed into the room.

'Sorry!' they said together.

'I was showing Samira my new ballet skirt,' explained Willow. 'Mum bought it on Saturday, on our way home from ballet. You know, the short floaty one that fits over my leotard. When I spin round, it swishes and swirls and feels great...'

'Yes, it is very pretty,' agreed Samira, though

she spoke more softly than usual.

'Hurry UP!' shouted Jake, 'or I'll be late and get told off. It will be all your fault. That's not fair!'

The next two days passed busily at school. There was a spelling test, and some new maths to learn, and the class did some interesting experiments with magnets. Samira still seemed very quiet, but Willow was, if anything, even noisier than usual.

'Just calm down, Willow love,' said her mum on Tuesday afternoon. 'You're getting over-excited. It's probably just a reaction to all the upset last week. But try to put that behind you, and look forwards. You've got a lot to learn at school this term *and* an awful lot of ballet. But we'll have to think of cutting back on ballet lessons if they're going to make you overtired and jittery...'

'Oh NO, Mum, NO!' Willow shouted. She rushed upstairs to her room, sat down hard on her bed, clenched her fists, and planted her feet firmly on the floor. She would show them! Of course she could cope with lots of schoolwork – and with lots of ballet!

Soon it was time to set off. Willow picked up her ballet bag and ran down to where her mother was waiting. It was only a short drive from their house to Rosewood Ballet School.

Determined not to seem tired, Willow jumped out of the car as soon as her mum had parked and switched off the engine.

'See you after class!' she called through the open car window, then ran off into the dusk. It was probably a good thing that she didn't look back; her mum's face had a rather worried expression.

Willow hurried through the entrance hall and headed for the changing room, pushing straight past Peter and Darren, who were chatting by the noticeboards, without even saying hello.

'Hey! Look out!' shouted Darren, as Willow whizzed by. He shrugged, and turned back to Peter. They were talking about Halloween; there were plans to hold a big firework display at the city football ground, and Darren's father was trying to get tickets.

'What's the matter with her?' Darren said, rather surprised. 'We're not late – there's plenty of time...'

Peter shrugged, too. 'Oh, you know what Willow's like; never still for a moment. She's a really nice kid; a good dancer and a good ballet friend, but sometimes... well... sometimes just a bit too busy!'

Jess and Gloria were already in the changing

room when Willow rushed through the door. As usual, Jess was struggling to tie her long curly hair into a neat ballet bun; as usual, Gloria was helping her. They were talking about the Saturday evening dance contest on TV.

'Did you see her footwork in that waltz?' asked Jessamy. 'It was fantastic! So quick and neat and precise – and keeping perfect time.'

She did a few graceful practice steps across the changing room floor: 'ONE–pom–pom, TWO–pom–pom, THREE–pom–pom.'

She laughed. 'Just look at me! Here I go – floating on air: TRAH–lah–lah–lah!' And she hummed a few bars from the famous 'Blue Danube' waltz that she'd heard from the TV.

'Well, she *is* a professional dance partner,' said Gloria, returning to the topic of Saturday's show. 'So she should be good. But it must have taken years of hard work to be able to dance like that – especially in such a long, heavy dress – and to guide that clumsy celebrity round the ballroom floor. It's hard enough to dance well alone, but *much* more difficult when the person you're dancing with keeps making mistakes... Whooah! Cool it, baby,' she laughed in a mock American accent, as Willow ran right up to them and flopped down on the bench beside Jessamy. 'Where's the fire?'

Willow frowned. 'No fire,' she said, ever so slightly offended. 'I'm just keen to get going. Miss Francisco said that we would start rehearsing our group dances today. I'm really looking forward to that!'

'Oh–kaaay,' said Gloria, cautiously. 'Great! That's cool! We'll wait until you've got changed, and then all go into the studio together. Darcey's late, as always, but I'm sure she'll join us when she's ready. Oh – and look! Here's Molly and Sophie just arriving. Hi guys!'

The warm–up exercises went well. With her hand resting lightly on the barre, Willow's feet moved neatly and quickly through *relevés*, *battements tendus* and *battements glissés*; away from the barre, she bounded lightly in the air in a series of *petits jetés*.

Relevé

'And rest!' Miss Francisco seemed quite pleased.

'Now, everyone – are you listening, Willow? Please stand still! I want us to start working on the 'grande finale' dance that you'll all do

together, right at the end of our performance.
You'll all start by taking up positions in rows
across the stage, as if you were stacked on
shelves in a supermarket, or in jars in an
old-fashioned sweetshop. Then Jessamy, our
Sugar Plum Fairy, will bring each of you to
life with a touch of her magic wand and do a
few steps with each of you in turn. After that,
you'll all swirl round the stage together in one
final dance, before running off through an open
space at the back of the stage that looks like the
doorway to a sweetshop… or perhaps like a big
paper bag.'

'Hmm!' thought Darren. 'My dad's very good
at helping to make scenery, but that is not
going to be easy…!'

Willow glanced across at Molly, raised her
eyebrows and pulled a questioning face.

Miss Francisco looked cross, but ignored her
and went on speaking. 'I've worked out new
steps for you all, but the music you will dance

to comes from the real Nutcracker ballet. It's a very pretty tune – listen…!'

She pressed the button on her CD player, and a lovely sweeping melody flowed out of the loudspeakers.

Quietly, so as not to disturb the others, Gloria hummed along. She had a good voice, sweet and tuneful: '*Laah–lah–lah LAAAAAH lah laaaaaah…*'

'That's right, Gloria,' said Miss Francisco, approvingly. 'It's good that you know the tune already – and that you are singing in time with the beat. The music is a waltz – a lovely, romantic dance – and, as I'm sure you know, waltzes always have three beats in a bar. Let's start the music again, and all count together. It will help you learn your dance. Here we go – join in with me, please! ONE two three, TWO two three, THREE two three…'

Together, the class hummed and counted, until Miss Francisco felt sure that they all could remember the rhythm.

'Now, in the real Nutcracker waltz,' she said, 'the dancers start off in pairs, with men and women in couples. But then they separate, and the female dancers move together to make lovely patterns on stage. We don't have many boys in this class, so I've based your new dance on that part of the Nutcracker waltz. The steps aren't difficult, but it's going to need a lot of careful counting – and concentration – to work together to make those patterns. We'll also need to work hard on your *port-de-bras*: the way you coordinate your arms with the movements of the rest of the body. We'll use your arms and fingers, together with your footwork, and the way you move your head and shoulders, to make beautiful flowing movements, to match the mood of the music. Let's have a little practice! Arms in first position – that's right, Darcey, a nice circle to front. Fingertips not quite touching, remember! Are we ready? To the count of three!'

Willow frowned with concentration as she listened to Miss Francisco calling out instructions.

'That's right!' Miss Francisco said. 'Open out first one arm – good! – look that way, then back to the centre. Now repeat with the other arm. Let your arms and fingers move smoothly, gently, as if they were floating on air. No sharp elbows, boys! Follow each movement of your arms with your head and eyes. When you dance, it's got to appear as if your whole body is being carried along by the music, from your toes to your fingertips...'

'Phew! That was hard!' thought Willow. All of a sudden, she was feeling really tired. Her thoughts began to wander, and – her heart sank – pictures of Samira's ruined garden flashed back into her mind.

'Pay attention please, Willow!' called Miss Francisco, before giving some more instructions. 'Now, shall we try our first few steps? As I said, your starting position will be in a line across the stage. Tallest people – boys and girls – in the middle, please. Smallest people at each end of the line. All I want to do this afternoon is to practise walking across the studio in time to the music, moving your arms and shoulders all together. Imagine that there are invisible strings linking your heads and hands...'

Willow tried hard, but she found it surprisingly difficult to coordinate her own lively movements with gentle, hesitant Molly on one side of her, and strong, confident Peter on the other.

'Just listen to the music, Willow,' called Miss Francisco. 'Follow the movements of your own hands with your eyes; try not to keep looking round at the people on either side of you.'

For once, Willow felt pleased and relieved when the class ended. She had an awful feeling that her friends were getting annoyed and impatient with her mistakes. They didn't say anything – they were her friends, after all. But, was she imagining it or did she glimpse Jessamy making a very critical grimace just behind her back?

Probably not. But she couldn't be sure.

Perhaps Willow's Mum had been right; perhaps she was getting too tired. 'But I *love* ballet,' she said to herself, as she pulled on her everyday clothes. 'It's my dream. I'm usually so good at it! What's going wrong?'

Later, back home, after something warm to eat – spaghetti, one of her favourites – Willow began to feel rather better. She even found herself humming the Nutcracker Waltz tune as she and Jake cleared away the dirty plates from the kitchen table.

'That's nice, Willow!' Their mum looked up from the nursing textbook she was reading. 'I think I know that tune! Isn't it from a ballet? Yes, *The Nutcracker*! I think it's called The Waltz of the Flowers.' She hummed a few bars, too.

'Now – homework, if you've got any, then early to bed for both of you. Willow, you look exhausted.'

That night, in her dreams, Willow saw lots of brightly-coloured sweets dancing on stage. They were followed by waltzing flowers.

Chapter 6

Worrying News

Brrriiiiing!!! Brriiiiinnnnng!!!

'Is that the doorbell? But it's only half past seven!'

Sid Johnson looked surprised. He was still sitting at the table, finishing his breakfast and, of course, reading a bike magazine. He put down his mug of tea and his knife – still covered with sticky marmalade – and started to get up.

'I'll go, Dad,' said Willow.

Before anyone could stop her, she hurried out of the room. She wasn't expecting to see Samira until she got to school; she knew that Mrs Khan would be taking Samira that morning, on her way to playgroup with Jamil. In spite of this, secretly, Willow hoped it might be her friend. But it was most unusually early for anyone to call round. So who could it be?

Willow reached the end of the hall and opened the heavy front door. Oh! It wasn't Samira, but the face that greeted her was friendly. And very, very talkative.

'Och! Good morning Willow,' said Kirsty MacTavish.

Willow's mum arrived at the doorway. When she saw who their visitor was, her anxious face relaxed into a smile.

'Oh it's you, Kirsty! Come on in!'

'I'm awfully sorry to be so early,' said Ms MacTavish, putting down her laptop bag and glancing at her watch. 'But I've to be at work soon after eight o'clock AND then I've got a big meeting this evening AND I have to catch the early Eurostar train to be in Brussels for a couple of days first thing tomorrow morning

AND I know that you sometimes work late on Thursdays AND I've got some news to tell you AND I thought you'd rather hear it sooner than later...'

She paused to catch her breath.

'Cup of tea?' offered Mrs Johnson, picking up the teapot.

'Thanks, but no thanks,' said Kirsty. 'I really can't stay long. But before I go away, I wanted to tell you what I heard last night. I bumped into Sergeant Evans – Hannah Evans, you know, the policewoman who came round here the other day to investigate all the damage. Yes, with blonde hair. Quite tall. Nice person, I thought. Very helpful and professional. Well, we were both at a meeting – another one – about community finances... So of course I asked her whether they had found out anything. It's early days, I know, but...'

'Are you sure you won't have a cup of tea?' said Willow's mum.

'No. No, thank you... Of course, Sergeant Evans couldn't say anything that might harm the progress of the police investigations, or interfere with any court case if the culprits are brought to trial later on. But she *did* say that we were not the only street where there had been damage, and that her colleagues had heard reports from another city – no, she didn't say where – about gangs who've been attacking corner shops and other small businesses. Afterwards, they put photos of the damage they've done on the internet, as if it were something clever. That's shocking, absolutely awful... Anyway, it seems they make these attacks partly to grab cash from shop tills – or for anything else they can steal, like Sid's fancy bikes, I suppose – and partly to attack people from...'

'Willow, will you go and make sure that Jake is eating his breakfast?' said Mrs Johnson, rather quickly. 'You know how slow he can be some mornings....'

'AND...' Kirsty MacTavish was eager to continue with her story, 'it seems that some local louts have started to copy these gangs, and even set up new gangs of their own. They don't just attack shops; they seem to be targeting anyone who doesn't have a local name and doesn't share their own hateful politics. It's bad – and very worrying.'

She gave a bitter laugh. 'It's not funny, and I'm not joking,' she said. 'But just sometimes I wonder to myself what these stupid gangs would make of a very Scottish name like MacTavish! After all, I'm an outsider – a newcomer to this city. I only moved here a couple of years ago. But Mr Patel and his family have run that shop for absolutely ages. And Mr Khan was born in the next street, I believe. He's lived and worked in this neighbourhood all his life. That must be at least 40 years. Now, before I go – Heavens, is that the time?! – I've

got something much more pleasant to tell you.
All our property was harmed – and, yes, some
was stolen – but nothing was so bad as the
damage to Samira's garden. That was terrible,
terrible… Poor wee lassie! So I've spoken to
several other women in the street, and we've all
offered to help Mrs Khan and Samira clean up
the mess and repair the damage and make the
garden just as beautiful as it was before. I've
been to see Mrs Khan, and at first she didn't
know whether she should agree to our plan. She
was a bit overwhelmed, I think.'

'Maybe she would prefer to do the work
herself…?' suggested Willow's mum. Kirsty
MacTavish meant well, but she wasn't always
very tactful. Sometimes, Mrs Johnson felt, she
was too busy talking to listen to other people.

'But there's such a lot to do!' replied Kirsty.
'I told Mrs Khan that the whole street had
admired her garden – even that scrappy
little patch in front of the house had some

lovely flowers, you know – and that's why her neighbours wanted to offer to help renew it. I said – and I think this is true for us all; it's certainly how I feel – that making a new garden would help us just as much as it would help her. It would be a good thing for the whole street. After that, she agreed. Most of us go out to work, so we don't have much spare time, but we'll take turns to help when we can; Mrs Khan can organise us and tell us what to do; as much or as little as she wants. I expect you'll want to help too, if you're not too busy?'

'Of course, so long as Mrs Khan really is happy with the arrangement,' said Josie Johnson. 'If so, then yes – add my name to your list.'

'Can I help, too?' asked Willow.

Her mum turned round sharply, with a little gasp of surprise. 'Willow! I didn't hear you come back! How long have you been standing there?'

'Oh, just a few minutes,' said Willow, rather

vaguely. 'Jake's had his breakfast.'

Later, at school breaktime, Willow and Samira were huddled side by side on a low wall in the playground. Willow was restless, as usual. Samira sat more quietly, but from time to time she could not help fiddling rather nervously with the ribbon that tied the end of her long, braided hair.

'I've been so worried about you,' said Willow. 'Though Mum says I shouldn't fuss. You're not feeling ill, or anything? Are you really all right?'

Samira smiled. 'You are such a kind friend, Willow! Yes, I'm OK. Honestly! Well, for most of the time. All my family are safe, and no one in the street got hurt. Not even Mr Big Ears! Those are the things that really matter. Of course I'm still sad about the garden, but – did you hear? – Mum's friends and neighbours are going to help us make a new one. Lots of people have offered to give us plants from their own gardens, or leftover packets of seeds. Mum cries a bit each time she thinks about how kind everyone is being. And she still gets very angry about the people who did all the damage. But mostly, I think, she's trying to forget, and making plans for the new garden. It will be fun, I think,' Samira's voice shook a little. 'Dad says he'll help me draw some designs for the garden using that new program on my computer. Oh Willow!' Samira suddenly hugged her friend very tightly. 'I miss my garden. Why did they spoil it? Why? Why? The new one will be nice, but it won't be the same.'

Willow did not – could not – answer.

Back home that evening, Willow stood in front of the big mirror on the front of the old-fashioned wardrobe in her parents' bedroom. She was trying to practise her arm movements, counting hard so that in the next rehearsal she could keep time with the music and with the other dancers.

She thought back to the last ballet class. What had Miss Francisco told them?

'Keep your head up, and follow the movements of your hands with your eyes...'

'Don't hunch those shoulders or lean over backwards...'

'Stand tall, but don't get tense... keep it graceful!'

'Your movements should be smooth and flowing...'

The words ran round and round in Willow's brain. The movements sounded simple, so why was she finding them so difficult to do?

Oh, if only Miss Francisco was there. Willow wanted help – that was one of her best qualities, she was always ready to learn. And she wanted help right now.

But she'd have to wait. Her next ballet class wasn't until after the end of school tomorrow. She felt tired just thinking about it.

Chapter 7

Too Much To Do

'The Friday class at Rosewood Ballet School had finished, and Willow had already gone home. She had danced quite well for most of the lesson, but clearly she was worried about something. She had concentrated ferociously on her steps all the way through each dance, with a frown on her face rather than her usual carefree smile. And Molly and Peter, who stood beside Willow in the Grande Finale dance, could tell that everything had seemed much more of an effort for her than usual.

When the class had finished, instead of hanging around to chatter with the other pupils as she usually did – or to mess about, making the others laugh, pulling funny faces in the changing room or doing cartwheels in the corridors – Willow had got changed quickly, said a quick and rather absent-minded 'Goodbye', and hurried to meet her Mum who was waiting in the car park outside.

Willow's best ballet friends – Darcey and Gloria – were still in the changing room. So was Jessamy. She was almost two years older than the rest of the class. Sometimes, she seemed rather too grown-up and annoying; tonight, Darcey and Gloria hoped she would be able to offer some sensible advice.

Jessamy pulled off the net that held her ballet bun in place, and tugged a brush through her unruly curls. She didn't offer advice in answer to the friends' question. In fact, she had a question of her own.

'Do you two know what's the matter with Willow?' she asked. 'Is she still upset about the attack on their street last week, or is it something more?'

Gloria was the first to reply. 'Yes, I think she is still upset,' she said, gently. 'Who wouldn't be after what her and her neighbors have been through? It must have been awful!'

She sat down beside Jess, and looked thoughtfully at her. 'But I think you're right. There's something else bothering her. I wonder...'

Suddenly, surprisingly, Darcey joined in. 'If Willow was my pet dog, I'd say that she was tired, or ill,' she suggested. 'Willow's usually such a bouncy dancer, full of energy. Today, her dancing was OK, but just, well, er, sort of normal...'

The other girls laughed, although it was not really funny.

'I'm sorry, that sounds stupid,' said Darcey. 'But do you know what I mean?'

The two girls nodded. Yes, they did.

'Miss Francisco has been telling Willow to calm down,' said Jessamy. 'Perhaps she's just overdoing it?'

'Well, that's possible,' Gloria agreed. But then she shook her head. 'No, I don't think it's that. Something else must be the matter. Poor Willow!'

'Do you think we should do anything?' Now Jessamy looked worried, too.

'No, not yet,' said Gloria. 'I'll try to find out what the problem is, and then perhaps we should tell Miss Francisco.'

'Hello, love,' said Mrs Johnson, as Willow opened her mum's car door. 'Did you have a good class? Did you dance well? How were Darcey and Gloria and Peter?'

'OK,' said Willow. She slumped down in the car seat and fastened the seatbelt. Her Mum looked across at her, rather sharply.

'No, it was fine, really, Mum,' said Willow, in a slightly brighter voice. 'I did all the dances quite well. Molly – she's next to me in the Finale – made LOTS more mistakes. We had to practise one bit over and over again, all because of her. Darcey and Gloria and Peter are fine.'

She gave a deep sigh. For the rest of the journey, she stayed silent.

'Willow, dear, what's the matter?' asked her mum, as she parked the car outside their house.

'Nothing, Mum!' said Willow. 'Nothing! What's for tea?'

It was Saturday morning and Mr and Mrs Johnson, just for once, were enjoying a peaceful breakfast together. Sid Johnson was in an exceptionally good mood; today he was going to buy a replacement bike for everyday journeys

and to look at some other, fancier bikes
designed for racing. Josie was simply relaxing
with the newspaper and a cup of tea. She
didn't often have the chance to sit down and do
nothing. Jake was out in the yard, talking to
his spiders. Sid Johnson had made a wooden
box on legs to house their vivarium, after he
had finished the new house for Mr Big Ears.

'Willow's still asleep,' said Mrs Johnson, 'and
I'm not going to wake her. She was tired out
after ballet last night, poor thing. I still wonder
whether these acting classes are too much
for her… on top of ballet and schoolwork…
Whatever's that?' She sat up suddenly, as a
burst of loud chatter and laughter, together
with the noise of clanging metal, floated
through the kitchen window. She got up and
peered out of the back door.

She came back, smiling broadly. 'It's Kirsty
MacTavish and that friend of hers we met
at her last Christmas party – Susan, I think

she's called. They've come to help Mrs Khan
and Samira in the garden. They've brought a
wheelbarrow, and forks and spades and what
looks like a pickaxe! I'm not sure what they
think they need that for… But right at the
moment, all they seem to be doing is standing
around gossiping and drinking mugs of tea!'

'Well, they've got a nice morning for it,' said
Sid. 'Now, if there's nothing more I can do here,
I'm off to the bike shop!'

Upstairs, Willow also heard the noises.
Curious, she clambered out of bed and came
downstairs.

'What's that, Mum?' she asked. There
was just a little note of panic in her voice. 'Is
everything OK…?'

'Hush, hush – it's all right, love, there's
nothing to worry about,' said Mrs Johnson. 'It's

just Kirsty MacTavish and a friend. They're out the back, helping Mrs Khan and Samira clear up the mess and make preparations for a new garden.'

Willow ran towards the stairs. 'I've got to get dressed so I can go and help them,' she said quickly, and hurried out of the kitchen. 'I'll be back in a minute...'

Mrs Johnson sighed, and rubbed her hand across her brow. 'Sometimes,' she thought to herself, 'it's not easy being a parent. I really don't want to upset Willow, or to disappoint her, and yet I'm going to have to. She simply does not have enough time – or energy – to start working on Samira's garden. She's only nine years old, after all! She has school work to do; it's important that she doesn't fall behind with lessons this term. And ballet classes, with grade exams coming up next year, and now acting classes, too... But Willow's a kind, helpful girl, and so of course she wants to help her friend, and Mrs Khan, as well. But I don't think she should. Not this time. Not now.'

Just a few minutes later, Willow bounced into the room. She was sensibly dressed in old jeans and even older trainers, with a scruffy jacket over a faded, baggy sweatshirt.

'Oh Willow,' said her Mum, feeling worse than ever. 'Just look at you. All ready to go... But' – and her voice grew suddenly serious – 'But honestly, love, I don't think you can. It will be too much for you. The sort of garden clearing they are doing right now is heavy work. There will be stones and big bits of wood, and broken glass. It's not a job for children. I don't think Samira's out there with them; I expect she's indoors, playing with Jamil. You were so tired yesterday after ballet, and you have another class this afternoon. And I'm sure you have homework...'

She looked at Willow's miserable face, and tried to think of something that might make her feel a bit better. 'In the spring,' she said, 'when your acting lessons have finished, and the ground is smooth and level, and Samira and Mrs Khan are ready to sow vegetable seeds and plant out little flowers, *then* you can go and help. That would be good, wouldn't it?!'

Mrs Johnson smiled what she hoped would be an encouraging smile. In Willow's place, she knew she'd be feeling upset and angry. 'And, later this afternoon, when you're back from ballet, why don't we ask Samira round for tea? You two can just take it easy and watch something nice on TV...'

'MUM,' shouted Willow, 'that will be too late! I want to help NOW!' She stamped her foot (Ow! It hurt!), burst into tears and ran out of the room.

As Willow stumbled up the stairs, Mrs Johnson heard her shouting again.

'Mum! You're so mean! Sometimes I HATE you!'

Willow did not want any lunch. She was still scowling and a bit sniffly when Sid Johnson, back from the shop and very happy with his new bike, drove her to Rosewood Ballet School for her acting class in the afternoon.

'Are you sure you want to go?' he asked as they drove into the car park. 'You can take an afternoon off if you're not feeling up to it. Missing just one session won't matter.'

'I don't want to miss anything,' said Willow. 'I want to go; it's really good. And,' she added, still angry, 'people at the ballet school aren't horrible to me.'

'Now come on, Willow,' said her dad. 'Be sensible. None of us can do everything we want to. Quite apart from anything else, there just aren't enough hours in the day. I'm sure Samira and Mrs Khan will understand. And, as your mum says, you can help them later. There's plenty of time.'

Willow went on scowling. Her dad went on speaking.

'Out you get, then, if you're going. I'll pick you up at 4 o'clock. Here, just outside the main doorway.'

'OK Dad,' said Willow. 'Thanks. I'll see you later.' And she scrambled out of the car.

It was only as Willow walked up the steep steps of the ballet school that she realised just how much her foot was hurting. It was the one she had stamped on the kitchen floor. Now every time she put her weight on it, sharp little stabs of something like fire flared up. But then, after a few seconds, they faded away.

Grimly, pressing her teeth together so as not to cry out with pain, she walked towards the studio where the Acting for Ballet class was about to begin.

Just as he had promised, Monsieur Philippe had brought in a DVD of *Swan Lake*. Together, the pupils watched the famous mime scene on screen, then gazed, fascinated, as Monsieur Philippe played the parts of the hunter-prince, the bewitched young girl and the frightened swan, one after the other.

'He's so good!' thought Willow. 'It's amazing how he can change from one character into the next. Just as he told us last week, he uses his whole body; he makes himself look so different for each part. I'd love to be able to do that, and I think I can, if I watch an expert like him, and practise hard enough.'

'Now, class!' said Monsieur Philippe. 'Here's your chance to be ballet actors! Choose a partner to work with, and then take it in turns to mime the prince and the young girl and the swan, while your partner plays the other parts, and mimes back at you.'

Willow's partner was Ruth. She was good to work with; serious but helpful. Willow tried standing up tall and proud, like the prince, with shoulders back, head high and chest out. As she did so, she felt a little twinge of pain.

'Not too bad,' she muttered to herself. 'Nothing to worry about.'

Soon after, it was Willow's turn to mime the frightened wild swan. As she'd learned in last week's class, she held her arms out like wings, fluttering her fingertips with fear. 'Good!' cried Monsieur Philippe. 'Very nice! Very expressive!'

Willow prepared to take a few cautious swan-steps towards Ruth, who was standing ready, looking nicely astonished, as the hunter-prince. She planned to stand on *demi-pointe*, balancing delicately, and then move by using several *pas couru* (tiny running steps) towards her partner. Counting time in her head, she stood ready to start, with her back foot firmly on the ground and her hurt foot, toes pointed, gently stretched in front of her. Then, as she slid her back foot forward, she shifted her weight on to her front foot and lifted her front heel from the floor. A sudden new pain – burning, stabbing, agonising – shot from her toes towards her ankle.

Willow screamed, and fell to the floor.

Chapter 8

Out of Action!

'Well, thank goodness nothing is broken.'

Josie Johnson helped Willow climb out of the car, and supported her as she limped through the front door and along the hall, then sank down wearily onto the sofa.

It had been a worrying few hours. Leaving her husband to look after Jake, Mrs Johnson had hurried to the ballet school as soon as Madame Olga had phoned, and had driven Willow to the nearest hospital with an Accident and Emergency Department. There they had waited – for quite a long time, but, as Willow's mum had explained to her, foot injuries were not life threatening. At last Willow's foot had been X-rayed and then checked by a senior nurse.

'Just a nasty bruise,' the nurse had said, 'and all that swelling will make it very painful. But in fact, you're quite lucky. It could easily have been what we call a stress fracture.'

Willow's mum nodded; she had learnt about those last term.

The nurse went on talking. 'A bruise will soon heal, but a fracture might have stopped you dancing for quite some time!'

Willow, who was already feeling rather weak and wobbly after no lunch, the acting class, and her collapse, had gone even paler.

'But the end of term performance?' she whispered. Her eyes threatened to fill with tears.

'That's several weeks away,' her mum had explained.

'Well, I want you to treat this foot gently

to begin with,' replied the nurse. 'Rest with your leg up for two or three days. Then, after that, try doing simple normal activities, such as walking around the house or the school playground. Maybe try a few ballet foot movements, too – but for the first day or so, do them sitting down! Go carefully, to begin with, and stop if the pain gets worse. No rushing around or rough sports. But if all goes well, I think you can start dancing properly again in about a fortnight. And, if necessary, I expect your ballet teacher will give you exercises to help rebuild the strength in that leg.'

'And,' she smiled at Willow's mum, 'I see you've got a nurse to look after you – and your foot – at home; that's even better. So cheer up! There's no lasting damage.'

'Thank you so much,' said Willow's mum, as the nurse hurried away from Willow's bed. 'Now, my poor hurt little dancer, it's time to get you home.'

The next day, Sunday, Willow felt better. She got up and got dressed, then came downstairs to sit on the sofa with her legs stretched out in front of her, and a ballet book to read. She felt even better when Samira and Mrs Khan called round in the afternoon to see how she was, then stayed to drink tea and juice and eat biscuits.

'Chocolate ones, as a special treat for our invalid,' said Willow's mum.

Willow and Samira tried out a new game on Samira's laptop, while Mrs Khan chatted with Mrs Johnson, and they both helped Jamil play with some old plastic building bricks that Jake still had in his bedroom.

After her visitors had gone, Willow found herself drifting off to sleep on the sofa. She didn't exactly dream, but images of Samira's garden and visions of waltzing flowers floated in and out of her mind.

Brrriiiiing! Brrriiiiing!

It was the doorbell again.

Willow's mum was in the kitchen. 'Oh, I do hope it's not Kirsty MacTavish again,' she thought, feeling rather guilty. 'I just don't have the energy this evening for a long conversation! Kirsty's a good neighbour, and I like her, but I just can't keep up with her, sometimes. It's exhausting! I've got supper to cook, then a chapter to read from a textbook online, and I need to make sure that the kids have everything ready for school tomorrow...'

But it wasn't Kirsty. Sid Johnson walked through the kitchen door, along with another – very welcome – visitor. Ruby and Gloria were such old friends of the Johnsons that they were almost like members of the family.

'Oh Ruby,' Mrs Johnson smiled with relief. 'It's you! Come along and sit down. We can chat while I'm cooking. Would you like tea, or coffee...?'

'No thanks,' said Ruby, sitting down. 'I can't stop for long; I'm on my way to meet someone. But I heard about Willow's foot, so I thought I'd just pop in and give her my good wishes.'

Ruby rummaged in her handbag. 'Also, I thought she might like this story to read. It's about boys and girls at a ballet school.'

She stood up again. 'I'll just say hello to Willow on my way out, then I must hurry.'

'But before I go,' she turned to look at Mrs Johnson, 'there's just one thing. Gloria said that even before Willow hurt her foot, she thought that something was upsetting her...'

Mrs Johnson sighed. 'It's so kind of Gloria to be concerned about her friends,' she said. 'And she's right, of course. Willow's not been her usual self for a while. I think she's got really overtired. Though she loves the acting lessons, on top of the ballet classes, they do mean a lot of extra effort for her. I've been wondering whether she should stop them.'

Mrs Johnson gave a worried frown, then continued.

'I think Willow would have coped OK, had it not been for what happened the other day in our backyards. She's recovered from the shock, I think, but she's really, really upset that we won't let her go with Kirsty MacTavish and the others to help rebuild Samira's garden. She wants to join in so badly. She feels terribly left out...'

Sid Johnson nodded. 'If only there were another, less tiring way that Willow could help with the garden,' he said. 'That might make her feel better.'

It was late afternoon on Tuesday and, as usual, the friends were arriving at Rosewood Ballet School: Peter, Darren, Molly, Sophie,

Oliver, Darcey, Jess, Gloria and the others. Everyone was there. Everyone except Willow.

'Her poor foot!' said Molly. 'It must have been awful.'

'Bad bruising happens to footballers, too,' said Peter. 'But they soon get over it.'

'We'll miss her when we rehearse the Grand Finale,' Sophie said, looking worried. 'It will be difficult with someone missing from the pattern.'

'Oh, but Willow will be coming back soon,' Gloria reassured them. 'At the end of next week, I think. That's what Ruby told me. She went round to see Willow and her mum the other day. Willow's doing well... I think she plans to go to school tomorrow. She can walk fine, though she limps a bit. But she's worried about missing dance classes.'

Later, in the changing room, Jess and Darcey came over to talk to Gloria.

'Did Willow's mum say anything to your
sister?' asked Darcey. 'You know, about why
Willow hasn't been dancing as well as usual?'

'I'm not quite sure,' said Gloria. 'But Ruby
did tell me something, and I think it's probably
important.'

'Ruby said that Willow has been very upset
about the damage to Samira's garden, and even
more upset that her mum and dad won't let
her help rebuild it. Willow's dad said that she
might feel better if there was something else
she could do to help Samira. But no one knows
what that might be. Willow's so busy. She's got
no time to spare!'

Gloria looked very thoughtful. 'There was
something else, as well. Willow told Ruby
that she keeps having dreams about dancing
flowers. They move in time to the Nutcracker
Waltz we've been learning. That's what you'd
expect, I suppose. But the flowers in Willow's
dreams aren't flowers from the ballet. They all

come from Samira's garden.'

Gloria stopped talking and looked at the other girls. 'What do you think?' she asked. 'I don't know what to do. Should we – or shouldn't we – tell Miss Francisco how Willow feels?'

Jessamy took the lead. 'Yes, I think we should. After this class, everyone?'

Darcey nodded. 'Yes. That's a good idea. I'll come with you.'

Brrrriiiinnnnng!

It was Friday evening and that was the doorbell, once again.

'More unexpected visitors!' said Mrs Johnson. 'My word! We are popular!'

She looked up from stacking the dishwasher.

'Willow, love, I'm rather busy,' she said. 'Go and see who it is, please...'

Willow's foot felt much better now, so, still

moving slowly and carefully, she made her way to the front door.

She opened it, and, to her amazement, found Miss Francisco standing there. Her teacher looked so different in an ordinary coat and jeans instead of her usual ballet skirt and leotard, that Willow had to blink a couple of times to make sure it was really her.

'Ah, Willow!' said Miss Francisco, smiling cheerfully. 'It's good to see you up and about. Are your parents in? I'd like to have a quick word with them. I phoned earlier on, and left a message. Perhaps your mother hasn't picked it up yet...?'

Mrs Johnson came to the door.

'Oh Miss Francisco! It's you! Come in, please, come in! What's that – a message? No, I've been working on a ward at the hospital all day and so my own phone has been switched off. Then it's all been rather busy since I got home... But it's nice to see you. Come on through, and sit down.'

'You come too, Willow,' said Miss Francisco. 'If that's all right with you, Mrs Johnson?'

Willow's mum smiled her agreement.

'Good,' said Miss Francisco. 'Because, Willow, I have an idea. An idea that I want to share with you.'

Chapter 9

Acting the Part

'And turn to face the front of the stage, and *galop, galop, galop*... Bounce on those toes! Good! Well done! Keep your movements light and airy... Now, Willow, Jessamy, Gloria! Let's go over your solos...'

It was two months after Willow had hurt her foot and six weeks since she'd been dancing again. And – Miss Francisco was delighted to see – Willow was once more moving to the music with all her old joy and passion.

Was it the fortnight's rest because of her hurt foot that had helped Willow feel – and dance – better? Or was it the chance to pour out all her feelings of shock and fear and anger in her dancing? Probably a bit of both, thought Miss Francisco, wisely.

Galop

Willow's friends were pleased, too.

'I'm glad that we went to see Miss Francisco,' said Darcey to Gloria, as they walked across the car park to where Darcey's dad was waiting to take them home. 'Though I nearly didn't come with you. I was very scared...'

'I was scared, too,' said Jess, hurrying along to catch them up.

Gloria joined in. 'I think Miss Francisco was already worried about the change in Willow's dancing, though she didn't say anything to us, of course.'

'But Miss Francisco didn't know how Willow felt about Samira's garden until you explained,' said Darcey. 'That was important! It helped her understand. I don't think Miss Francisco's ever met Samira, has she?' Darcey continued. 'Samira's nice, and, even better,' Darcey gave a wicked grin, 'like quite a few people I could mention, she's just not interested in ballet.'

She pointed to herself in a really rather good ballet mime.

Gloria laughed. Everyone knew that Darcey wasn't ballet mad, like the rest of them.

Jess interrupted. 'But then, once Miss Francisco knew about the attack on Samira's garden, it didn't take her long to come up with a brilliant idea. I'd never have thought of it, would you?'

The two friends shook their heads, together.

'It's great that Mrs Khan liked the idea, as well...' said Jess. 'That made it all possible.'

'And Ruby didn't mind altering the costumes, once she knew the reason,' said Gloria. 'Did your mum complain, Darcey?'

Darcey smiled. 'Oh, Mum loves anything to do with ballet – the more she can get involved with, the better! Anyway, at least the music has stayed the same, and many of the solo dances... Oh look! There's my dad's car. Come on, Gloria. See you at the next rehearsal, Jess. Byeeee!'

Monsieur Philippe walked briskly and neatly into the ballet studio, and gave his usual wide smile to the pupils. This time, he was taking the Friday afternoon dancing class, alongside Miss Francisco.

'Are we all here? Good! Then let's begin! Let's all do our very best in this extra special lesson!'

Willow jumped up and down with excitement – she just could not stand still. Her foot was fine, with not the faintest painful feeling. Darcey, Gloria and Jess all looked happy, too.

Monsieur Philippe went on speaking.

'As you know, for your end of term performance you're no longer being cakes and candies. No! Instead, you're lovely fruits and flowers. Miss Francisco has decided that most of your dance steps should stay the same. There's no time to learn new ones and,

I expect...' he gave a broad wink and a smile, 'I expect that very few people know whether a toffee or chocolate drop dances differently from an apple or a buttercup.' The class giggled.

'And so this afternoon,' Monsieur Philippe continued, 'I want to help you with a few simple mimes, to help express the new characters you are dancing. We have roses, yes? I want you to be elegant, poised, graceful. You know you look good and smell sweet. Your challenge is to show that in your movements! And climbing, twining honeysuckle? We must have those arms in really twisty, clinging poses.' Monsieur Philippe wrapped his long slender arms around himself, swaying dramatically. 'And we have some jolly daffodils? And cheerful daisies? Good, good! Your task is to show the pleasure of a sunny spring day. Now, daisies – Molly and Sophie, isn't it? – remember, all your movements need to be really neat and dainty, like the tiny petals of a daisy flower. Lift your faces and smile up towards an imaginary sun. That's great! Lovely! Next, who's our tree? With waving branches? Hmm! That's very nice, Oliver. And our tomatoes? Keep that footwork tidy, and mime being plump and soft and very, very red...'

Darren sniggered.

'Actually, I meant that,' said Monsieur Philippe. 'Think red! See if you can communicate feelings of glowing heat and energy. Try, and you might be surprised! Now then, who are our cabbages? I want you to look tough and sturdy on stage. Keep all your movements rounded, like big fat cabbage leaves. You are tall! You are proud! You are strong! Well done, Darren. See – it can be done! Ah Peter! Where are you? Your solo follows the cabbages, and then you come back and chase them and you all dance together. You bend and stretch and wriggle, just like you did in your old chewing gum dance. But this time, we need more. We want to see you miming "food" and "hungry"! Because now...' Monsieur Philippe suddenly crouched down and arched his back, then slithered along the floor. The ballet class burst out laughing, then clapped their hands. He looked so funny! 'Because now, Peter,' said Monsieur Philippe, who was also laughing and still stretched out on the ground, 'now you are our big, hungry, greedy caterpillar!'

Chapter 10

Samira's Garden

Willow and Samira were sitting side by side in Mrs Khan's kitchen. Jamil was playing with a very noisy book on the rug nearby. It had bright, cheerful pictures of animals – a cow, a cat, a sheep, a duck and a mouse. Each time Jamil pressed a picture, the book made a matching sound. Jamil thought this was wonderful, but it meant that the girls were interrupted all the time by loud and unexpected animal voices. Having a serious – or even a calm and thoughtful – conversation was proving impossible.

'Samira,' said Willow. 'Do you think...?'

'MOO!' said Jamil's book. 'BAA! MIAOW!'

Jamil laughed delightedly.

'This is getting ridiculous!' exclaimed Samira. 'Let's go outside. I'll just tell Mum that we're no longer keeping an eye on Jamil.'

'MIAOW!' said the book, again. 'SQUEAK! MOO! QUACK!'

Willow waited with Jamil until Mrs Khan bustled into the kitchen, then the two girls went out into the backyard. It was cold, but not raining. Almost, but not quite. Willow shivered.

All around, she could see traces of the gardening work that Kirsty MacTavish and her friends had been doing with Mrs Khan.

'Look,' said Samira. 'Here are our new rose bushes. They look rather dead now, but Mum says they will grow fine. And in spring, this is where we'll have some grass and more flowers. And last weekend, though it is a bit late, Mum planted a hundred new daffodil bulbs...'

She turned to Willow, who was looking rather pale. 'Are you OK?' she queried. 'Yes, I'm just cold,' said Willow. 'It is December!'

'So what was it you wanted to ask me?' said Samira. 'I'm sorry to bring you outside, but I just couldn't think straight with all Jamil's noise. We can go inside again, if you want?'

'No, wait...' Willow took a deep breath, and turned to face her friend. 'Samira, I know that you don't like ballet, but will you come and watch me dance next week, with all my ballet friends?'

Samira looked surprised.

Willow hurried on. 'My mum has asked your mum, and they both say it's OK. You see...' she took another deep breath, 'you see, for our end of term concert, we've been practising a new little ballet. It's all about flowers and vegetables and growing things. It's called... well, um, er, well – it's called Samira's Garden!'

Samira stepped back. 'A ballet? About me?' She looked startled and not very pleased.

'No, no, not about you.' Willow's words came

tumbling out in her hurry to explain. 'It's about the garden. After the attackers came to our backyards, I wanted to help you make your new garden, but Mum said no because I was too busy, with school and ballet and acting. So I got upset and couldn't dance properly and I felt awful. And after I hurt my foot, Miss Francisco heard about your garden. I don't know how. She came to see me and said she thought that it might be a nice idea to change the ballet we'd been planning – if you remember, that was all about sweets. Instead, Miss Francisco said, why not do a ballet about flowers, and fruit, and your garden?'

Willow paused for breath, 'After all, the music we'd been learning to dance to is called the Waltz of the Flowers. I've tried to keep it a secret. That's not been easy, and I think I've probably showed you some of the steps over the past few weeks, when we've been playing after school. But it's been cold and dark outside, so I've not done much practice there, and inside both our houses there's not much room for dancing. So you won't have seen a lot, I suppose... The ballet was meant to be a nice surprise for you. But if you're not happy...'

Willow's lower lip trembled and she seemed about to burst into tears.

Samira flung her arms around her friend. 'Oh Willow! Don't cry!' she said. 'Now I understand what you mean, of course I don't mind! It's a lovely idea.'

'But I'm not getting up on stage,' Samira said, suddenly looking very stern. 'No way! Never! Not even for you, my best friend! But of course I'll come and watch you dance. When will it be? And where?'

'It's funny,' thought Willow, 'I'm not usually nervous like this before a performance. Everyone feels a few butterflies in their stomach, of course. That's only natural. But this time, I'm really, really scared.'

It was a week or so after Willow had told Samira about the new ballet. Miss Francisco's class were in the dressing rooms at the little, dusty, shabby old Royal Theatre. In fact, it wasn't much bigger than the assembly hall at Willow's school, but it had lovely old-fashioned red theatre curtains, and a slightly springy wooden stage that felt really good to dance on.

The class had all done their hair and had their faces painted with stage make-up. Now they were waiting in their dressing gowns while Ruby and Darcey's mum helped them into their costumes for their solo dances. Those came first, then some pupils – the better dancers, like Willow – changed to do a second solo before they all danced together in the Grand Finale.

'I know all my steps,' Willow said to herself, ticking off a list of movements on her fingers. She tried a few gentle jumps, but there was not much room backstage.

'Try to keep still, Willow,' called Miss Francisco. 'Save your energy for your performance.' But she wasn't cross; her voice sounded kind and she smiled.

For her first solo dance, Willow was dressed all in green.

'There, all done! You make a lovely vegetable!' laughed Ruby, as she checked that Willow's headdress – a wreath of green leaves – was secure. Miss Francisco had cleverly changed Willow's dance as a rolling, jumping chocolate button into a lively fresh garden pea.

Willow had practised every day; not just her ballet steps but also the mime gestures that Monsieur Philippe had taught her. She made round movements with her eyes, her mouth, her head, her hands and her toes, to show the round shape of a pea. She finished her dance with cartwheels across the stage, like a pea rolling over the ground. It took a lot of energy, but, when it worked, it was a lot of fun.

'I hope Samira likes it,' thought Willow. 'I wonder if she's out there in the audience by now? Mum and Dad will be bringing her, together with Jake, of course. And Monsieur Philippe is going to make a recording of the whole performance, so that Mr and Mrs Khan and other parents who aren't here can see it at home. It's such a pity that Mr Khan had to drive his ambulance this afternoon, so they couldn't come. But Samira can tell them all about it – if she thinks it's any good, of course.'

So that was it! Now Willow understood. She was feeling extra nervous because her best friend would be watching... She gulped, and clasped her hands to her chest. The butterflies did a frantic dance inside her. 'Will I really be OK...?'

Just in time, before Willow made herself thoroughly sick with nerves, Miss Francisco's clear voice rang round the dressing room.

'Beginners in position on stage, please! And all other solo dancers ready in the wings. Curtain up in five minutes! Come along, Willow! Time to go!'

Hop, skip, cartwheel, cartwheel, *pas courus* to the front of the stage, then a deep curtsey to the audience.

It was over! She had done it! There had been one or two ragged steps, but – hooray! – Willow's first solo had gone well. Panting with excitement as well as effort, she stood as gracefully as she could, curtseyed again, and peered ahead, past the thick red curtains.

Could she see her mum and dad? No!! A moment of panic. But then, ah, yes! They were over there. And Samira was with them. She was talking to Jake. What was she saying? Had she liked it? Well, the pair of them were laughing and smiling...

Now time to get changed for the second solo and finale. Still feeling a bit nervous, but rather more hopeful, Willow pattered off to the dressing room, where Darcey's mum was waiting for her.

'Well done Willow! Let's get you out of that greenery and into the next costume,' she said. 'But first of all, I've got something for you. As soon as she got to the theatre this evening, your mum asked me to give it to you. You know the rules. Only approved helpers are allowed backstage – no wandering in and out by friends or family. So I'm afraid I was too busy to give it to you straight away. But here it is, now.'

Darcey's mum handed Willow an ordinary-looking envelope. Willow didn't recognise the handwriting. Who could it be from? Puzzled, she tore open the flap – and then, what was this?! A glittery card with a picture of lovely flowers on the front, and inside – wowee! – a ticket for Willow to go on Madam Olga's school trip to see the real Nutcracker performance danced by world famous ballet stars!!

Willow gasped. 'Oh!' She could hardly speak. 'This is amazing!... I never thought I'd be able to go!'

She got her breath back, brushed some prickly glitter from her fingers, then wondered aloud. 'But I don't understand... Who sent it?'

She looked at the card again. Inside, there was a short and simple message.

'To Willow,' it said, 'from all the Khan family.'

Miss Francisco hurried in. 'Willow!' she said. 'Don't just sit there in a dream, though it's nice to see such a lovely smile on your face. Get changed. Now! It's nearly time for your next dance.'

Quickly, Darcey's mum helped Willow into her second costume. It was red this time, and a billowy shape – very difficult to dance in. Concentrating as hard as she could, though her mind was still in a whirl, Willow tried to remember all the steps of her solo. Monsieur Philippe had helped her with the mime for this dance, too. She must try to do her best for him. And she mustn't make a fool of herself...

Gently, but firmly, Miss Francisco ushered Willow into the wings. 'You're next,' she said. 'Good luck! Dance well!'

The applause – and happy laughter – for Peter's caterpillar solo died away, and the music for Willow's dance started.

'I really hope Samira likes this,' Willow thought, as she raised her arms in a graceful arched shape, and skipped lightly on stage. 'I hope she sees the joke. If not, she'll tease me for ever and ever! Now, I must concentrate! Count the beats... Waltz, waltz, ONE two three, TWO two three... Feel the music! Mime! Sweet and beautiful, and pink and fragrant... This is either my best – or my very worst – dance ever. It's the dance Samira said would never happen. Yes, that's right: it's the Dance of the Squashy Strawberries!!'

The end

The Nutcracker: The Story Behind the Ballet

The *Nutcracker* ballet was first performed in St Petersburg, Russia, in 1892. Its storyline was inspired by a strange and sinister tale, *The Nutcracker and the Mouse King*, by German fantasy writer, E.T.A. Hoffmann (1776–1822). However, the plot of the ballet did not follow that story very closely, and, over the years, ballet companies have made many more changes. Even the names of some characters have been altered – for example, in the USA and in Russia, the young heroine is often called Marie or Masha (a Russian version of Mary). In the UK she is known as Clara.

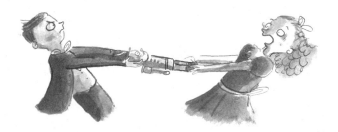

The original dances for *The Nutcracker* were showy and spectacular. They were suggested by famous dancer and choreographer Marius Petipa (1818–1910), who created several of the world's best-known ballets, including *Giselle* and *The Sleeping Beauty*. But he fell ill and the actual work of choreography was carried out by his deputy, Lev Ivanov.

The directors of the Imperial Theatre in St Petersburg asked the admired Russian composer, Pyotr Illich Tchaikovsky (1840–1893), to write the music for the ballet. From its first performance, Tchaikovsky's music was praised as 'rich… inspired… beautiful, melodious, original…' Today, it is still very popular – and even better known than *The Nutcracker* ballet.

The story of *The Nutcracker* takes place
at Christmastime, and, in many countries,
especially the USA, it has become traditional
to stage performances of the ballet every
Christmas. Often, these shows are designed for
young audiences; many ballet lovers say that
The Nutcracker was the first live ballet they
ever saw – and that they liked it so much, they
wanted to see more.

In some ways, this is surprising, as the story of *The Nutcracker* has often been criticised. After the first performance, people said it was 'confusing' or 'unbalanced'. (The first act tells the story of Clara and the Nutcracker Prince; the second act is mostly a collection of unconnected dances.) But in other ways, the music and dances of *The Nutcracker* are just so amazingly good that they seem to weave a spell over audiences, carrying them away to an enchanted land. And that's part of the magic of ballet!

The Nutcracker

It's Christmas Eve! Time for a party!

Clara and Fritz get
dressed in their best
party clothes.

Their guests start
to arrive.

The big, handsome
clock strikes 8.

And who's this? It's
Drosselmeyer –inventor,
toymaker and magician!

He brings amazing
presents: life-size
talking dolls!

They're too
fragile to
play with.

We must put
them away.

Another present! A nutcracker shaped like a
handsome young man.

No! He's mine!

Fritz is jealous and argues with his sister...

SNAP!

CRACK!

Later that night, Clara creeps downstairs.

'Poor broken Nutcracker!' she thinks sadly.

The clock strikes midnight.

Who's this? Drosselmeyer! He waves his magic wand...

Clara's astonished! The tree, the toys, the mice and the Nutcracker are all much, much bigger!

The Nutcracker fights the Mouse King.

Clara throws her slipper at the Mouse King.

The Nutcracker turns into a Prince.

The Prince invites Clara to his kingdom.

The Prince takes Clara to visit the Kingdom of Sweets. They meet its Queen, the Sugar Plum Fairy.

The Sugar Plum Fairy asks her sweets to perform a dance for Clara.

Glossary

Battement glissé
The same as battement tendu (below), but quickly sliding the foot into position while lifting the toes a little way off the ground.

Battement tendu
Stretching one leg out to the front or side of the body or behind. The toes of that leg are pointed, but stay on the floor.

Demi-plié
Lowering the body, keeping the back straight and both knees gently bent.

Demi-pointe
Standing on the balls of your feet.

Developpé
Moving one foot, toe pointed, up to the knee, then extending or 'unfolding' the rest of that leg, raising it high and keeping it straight. A smooth, controlled movement, not a big kick.

En pointe
Dancing on the tips of the toes, in specially stiffened 'pointe' ballet shoes.

Fouettés
Steps where one leg 'whips' round.

Galop
A step for moving quickly across the floor. Swing one leg forward, toe pointed, and then jump, bringing both feet together in the air. Land with your knees gently bent (demi–plié) and then swing the front leg forward again.

Pas couru
Tiny running steps.

Pas-de-deux
A dance duet where two dancers, usually male and female, perform steps together.

Petit jeté

Start with one foot raised, toes pointed and touching the muscles of the calf at the back of the other leg, then jump from one foot to another. Don't move position; try to stay on the same spot on the floor.

Relevé

Moving from both feet flat on the floor to standing on tiptoe.

Relevé

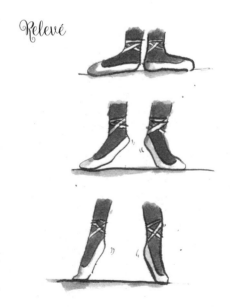